More Than Forever

Kate Sparrows

Publisher's Note: This is a work of fiction. Names, characters, places, and incidents are a product of the author's imagination. Locales and public names are sometimes used for atmospheric purposes. Any resemblance to actual people, living or dead, or to businesses, companies, events, institutions, or locales is completely coincidental.

Cover Design: Melody Pond; http://melodyypond.weebly.com
Printed by CreateSpace, An Amazon.com Company

More Than Forever/ Kate Sparrows. -- 1st ed.
ISBN 978-1-943797-06-6

For Monica, who made me promise not to kill anyone.

I, well...

Prologue

Three years.

Three years had seemed like a long enough time to get over her. It seemed like a long enough time to find myself again. It seemed like a lot of things, yet here I was. The same person as when I left. I was even bringing the same flowers to her grave. Orchids and jasmine. Beauty and strength, and love. Two flowers that seemed so opposite but ended up perfect for her.

I trace her stone carved name – Ava Koltrin – and imagine how things could have been. Our baby would be turning three in a month, probably. She would have taken after her mother and been a handful. There was no way to know what we would have had, but a girl always seemed right. It seemed like the only image I could picture in my head was being sandwiched between two beautiful, smiling girls. And yet it's one thing I will never have.

Even being here at Ava's grave feels like something that I can never have, at least completely. For three years, I've tried to leave. Not her, but the man I was. I've forced myself to get lost as I drove through the wilderness of Canada and to let go as I hung upside down to kiss a rock in Ireland. I even pulled on a grass shirt and a coconut bra to wiggle my hips, completely sober, in Hawaii. I've traveled. I've seen things, ate things, learned things. Yet it didn't seem enough to find what was missing, and every year I returned here to find something missing as well.

Ava had completed me wholly. There wasn't an ounce more that I was missing or left to want. At the one place I thought this feeling of loneliness and longing would leave was here, at her grave – the one place where she was left on this earth. And yet, it felt the emptiest.

Chapter One

"I don't know, mom. It's something I never really thought about."

Sure it had been three years, but it was understandable that they were anxious to know what I was going to do. They had tried so much to deflect Ava's death and make life more manageable, at least after the media broke the news. When I was forced to take a "voluntary" separation from the company, they believed it meant I was moving back home, not taking off across the country and roaming Europe. After losing Ava and then my job, moving back home felt like too much of a do-over. I wanted to move on, not rewrite.

"Jack, we're only three hours away. If you want to visit the big city you can, but you should be with family. You've dealt with so much, let me take care of you." I knew my mom had good intentions, but it just felt too much. It was getting exhausting to have to explain this over and over, without her understanding. "You can relax or get a job back at Baker's. You used to like working there with the tools and putting things together."

"Mom," groaning I plopped down on the couch, "I was thirteen and it was my first job and Mr. Baker let me play with the power tools. Of course I like it." The pay had been great for a teenage boy with no financial needs and a slight god complex. "And I don't think Mr. Baker wants me back, even if he had a job open."

Crap. Was that why she called? I knew my mom was a crafty one, but clearly it was just something that came up randomly. As much as she wanted me home, she wouldn't go behind my back to get me a job that I didn't want. At least that's what I thought.

"Honey, I already talked to him and he'd love to get you back. You were great with putting together those furniture kit things. He says you can start anytime, so as soon as-"

"There's one more place I have to go," I cut her off. It's not often that I do. Then again, it's not often that's she's pushing – no, forcing – me into something.

"Oh." She seems shocked. Clearly she expecting a different response, probably for me to refuse and argue it. Perhaps that would have been the easier choice. Instead, I had lied and knew my time was short until she asked. "Where are you going, Jack?"

That was the million dollar question. I had tried to find myself in the middle of nowhere, to find love where it was just a drunken pub away, and I was still stuck. And Ava wasn't around this time with her clues to point me in the right direction. I was a broken compass that never pointed north.

"I was thinking somewhere different." It wasn't an answer, but I needed to buy time. Without being able to think of a single place, surely I'd be stocking shelves and piecing together furniture by the end of the month. Glancing at the coffee table, careful to avoid hitting anything as I propped my feet up, I noticed a CD case poking out under yesterday's newspaper. The crow on the front made me realize it was Ava's before noticing it was a Train album. They had been her favorite band, and I tried so hard to learn all their songs as I dashed through airports and drove along the roads to nowhere. My mom was waiting for an answer and when I flipped the case over, I had it.

Save Me, San Francisco.

It felt like a sign. Ava's favorite band. Needing to be saved. A city I could tell my mom. "San Francisco."

The phone was hushed.

"Sounds like a good place, honey... Hey, your father just walked in. Do you have anything to say to him?" I can't believe that she's buying it; yet, at the same time, I know she's stuck between a rock and a hard place. Who is she to say when my mourning will be over? And maybe San Francisco will be exactly what I need. My dad would be another story entirely.

"Just tell him that I say hello."

Saying our goodbyes, we disconnected. "San Francisco..." It was a town I had looked at. Besides the Golden Gate and Alcatraz, there was nothing there. I'd rather head to Old City in Philly and grab a lager at a pub or listen to some rustic Italian, maybe even venture down South Street for something adventurous. It was beyond me what possibly could be offered in some hippy town on the other side of the country. But, having just told my mom that's where I was going, it looked like I was going to find out firsthand.

Ava, why do you hate me?

How can it be in the high 60s, low 70s at the end of August? The weather didn't make sense. It was California. Sun. Hot. Glamorized by celebrities. This was hardly what I expected. The eight and a half hour flight was one thing, but the weather when I landed at San Francisco International Airport was another. I also hadn't imagined landing in the middle of nowhere in what looked like plains. It was a big place for having nothing around.

I grabbed my checked bag and followed the arrows that lead to the train. A train; now that was something I knew. It was strange to walk through a parking garage to get there, but it seemed like the only route. With the building just off the terminals, it didn't seem like a bad walk. Ten minutes max. There were a few other brave souls heading my way too. Although once I wound my way up the ramps to the platform, they disappeared when I realized that the pay card system was like none I've seen before. The machines reminded me of the New York subway, but the fare portion was more Washington DC Metro.

I saw my train come and go before I could even get a card. Maybe this had been a poorly planned decision. I had gotten excited and curious to see their transit system, BART. A taxi would have saved so much hassle in getting to this hotel on Sutter Street, even though the reviews boosted of the ease using BART to get there. This wouldn't have been a problem if Ava had come along with her foresight. We'd probably be in downtown San Fran right now having an adventure on a cable car.

By the time the next train arrived, a half hour later, I had been successful in reaching the platform with my fare card. I must have been a sight with my face against the glass doors of the platform area, ogling over the trackwork and power systems. I wish I could have enjoyed the scenic ride through South San Fran with as much enthusiasm as I had the transit system. The mission churches, rolling hills, architecture... it was all lost on me. The only thing holding my attention, parallel to nothing but Ava, was a huge man sporting a fishnet tank and a rainbow Mohawk on the other side of the car from me. "Tiny", somehow, had a more interesting pet with him. On the floor sat a svelte woman with beautiful chocolate waves and piercing blue eyes. If it wasn't for the studded dog collar, leash and ball gag, I would have never guessed she was anything but normal with her dark washed jeans and white tee.

Toto, we're not in Kansas anymore.

When the train hit Montgomery Street Station, I couldn't dash away fast enough. If only that was to be the strangest sight the city had to offer. A few homeless littered the area up to street level, and it was obvious who the tourists were that crowded the street. Getting pass the Grateful Dead and alternative lifestyles, the city had a certain special kind of beauty. Now if only these streets made sense.

The city blocks were standard rectangles unlike the twisty, windy streets of Boston or the radial layout of Washington DC. All I needed to do was find Kearny Street. Kearny would lead me right to Sutter, and if I went too far I'd end up in the Bay. With the block in front of me a triangle with probably less than a hundred square feet, there was a risk of completely missing the right one. Luckily from my post, I could see the street sign just on the other side of my little unique city block – Geary, Kearny, Market Streets.

Moving to step across the street, though, brought another surprise. The dinging bells of a street car alerted me to another culture shock. Sure, in Philadelphia, there were street cars and city buses that didn't care what was in front of them but this was entirely a new experience. There wasn't a doubt in my mind that I was going to ride one, and here I thought the cable cars were the only interesting thing.

The hotel was tucked away a little, about halfway down Sutter. From the outside, it looked like a typical high-rise building but, inside, the décor and architecture was stunning. It brought back the feeling of the roaring twenties and the brilliance that must have been the technology boom. I hadn't expected this from my first impressions. Surrounded by modern... everything, this was a gem. A sign at the front desk – Nightly Local Wine Tasting – caught my eye and I wish Ava could have been here with me. This would have been in the top five places for what could have been our honeymoon. And to think that in a few months it would have been four years since I would have asked her.

I watched another guy strike out. As much as I felt myself assuming the worst about this girl – that she was a bitch or a lesbian or a girl using the male attention for her own kicks – I couldn't help but think she deserved to. The blonde was beautiful. Her hair cut in an adorable bob and pinned up in that sexy but effortless way that I was sure took hours to achieve. Pair that up with a golden tan, white fringe vest and daisy dukes, there was no avoiding it. Everything with a pulse was going to take notice. There was no way I couldn't, and no way I couldn't give it a try too. Striking out didn't really seem so bad when I was just a tourist, bound to never see her after tonight.

Scooting out of my booth, I headed over to her at the bar. "So what do they call you?"

I had been too far away to hear any bit of her previous five conversations, but starting with her name seemed logical. I knew that I wasn't smooth enough to start calling her babe or sweetheart the whole time we talked. *If* we talk that is.

"They call me a California dime."

Her voice was so sweet and nice that I almost missed her trying to blow me off. I had to be just another face tonight, and surely not the last to try and talk to her. It was just... "What's a California dime?"

"It means I'm too hot to talk to."

She sighed. "It means there's going to be a line of guys behind you, all thinking they're better than you and they won't hesitate to tell you that. They see you talking to me and they'll kick you out before I even have to tell you that I'm not interested."

It was as if she could read my mind. Then again, I never was very good at keeping secrets. Well, at least from showing on my face. Ava always managed to read me and get the upper hand. I watched as she casually took a drink from some orange-red drink.

"Well, I'll just have to take my chances that the next guy doesn't beat me up too badly. I'm a really bad fighter. I'd probably scream like a girl." Unfortunately, that was probably true. "And I don't care if you're this dime thing. You just looked nice and I thought, with you sitting alone, that you might be lonely."

One skeptical glance was enough to tell me she thought it was some cheesy pick-up line and it kind of sounded like it. "My name's Jack. And maybe I'm the one that's been sitting by myself, kind of lonely, and having no idea why I'm in this bar or even in this town."

"You don't know why you're in this town?" A thin blonde eyebrow rose, as if doubting me but intrigued.

I sighed. "I kind of spontaneously decided to come here to avoid some stuff back home and I have no idea what I'm doing. I have no idea what to do here. Not even the touristy crap that I'm sure everyone else here's for." The way she downed her drink and seemed to be looking for the nearest exit clued me in. "I'm not running from some bad stuff... just my parents. They've been after me to move back in with them and I've been avoiding them by traveling the last few years. Honestly, what kind of trouble do I look like I could have gotten into?"

It got her to pause, and even try to cover up a laugh. "You do seem like a mama's boy." She still got off the bar stool and grabbed her bag. "Have you been on the cable cars?"

"Yes..." Was she actually going to talk to me? Maybe I had misread things and she was going to head back to my booth.

"Take the Powell-Hyde line to the last stop tomorrow. Bring forty dollars." She smiled, moving towards the door. "And I'll see you at two, Jack."

I watched her walk out, not having a single clue as to what just happened. Did she... were we... was this a date? And why forty bucks? Forty bucks seemed like such an odd request. Maybe it wasn't a date. I head back to my booth as my chicken strips arrive. It was more than a disappointment that I didn't get her number, and surely it'll make it harder to find her tomorrow. *If* she shows. I pull up my map application on my phone and try to figure out where that lands me. The whole two times that I rode the cable cars, I've hit it when the Powell-Mason line was rolling in. With it stopping a couple blocks from Fisherman's Wharf – the tourist epicenter – I hadn't thought about what I might be missing out on with the other line.

Following the map of the cable routes, they split a block from each other by the Cable Car Museum. Now that's not something I've been to, and I hadn't even realized it was there. That definitely was going to be a spot I hit up, but it wasn't the spot the blonde mentioned. The end of that line was at Hyde Street, a short walk to Fisherman's Wharf on the west side. It looked like the

Ghirardelli Chocolate Factory was there and a path along the Bay to the bridge. Was she going to have me take her shopping or shake me down for a couple twenties?

It was obvious that she was a local or at least someone that's been here a while. She probably knew this city like the back of her hand, and here I almost insulted her by pointing out how there's nothing. And two o'clock? That was kind of an odd time to grab lunch, or really do anything. It was looking like I'd have to resign until tomorrow to find out. But there was still the chance that this "California dime" was blowing me off like the slew of men at the bar. There was no damage done in planning a day in case she stood me up, but I hoped she wouldn't. She hadn't looked the type at first, but those daisy dukes were probably a sign she was a seasoned heartbreaker.

Chapter Two

The line of tourists at Powell Street was ridiculous. It wrapped around the turntable and up two blocks on the other side of the street from where you boarded. Maybe I should have left sooner. I had figured forty minutes would be enough time to get up there. How wrong was I? It made me nervous to stand in line, knowing how limited the space was on the single cars and how long before another departed. Add in how they alternated between the two lines, I could be an hour late and there was no way to let her know. There was nothing to do but wait behind a gaggle of tourists that didn't have a clue, that couldn't even pay attention to see the line was moving. They were all distracted by the street performers with their tricks and nice voices, all asking for some coins. I was getting more anxious as the minute hand on the plaza clock was getting closer to the top.

Five minutes. There was no way that I was going to make it there in time. I don't know if it was a peak time or if the service was increased to the weekend, but I was one cable car away from being on my way. If only I knew a shortcut and had the stamina, I'd run there. If I could manage to sneak on this next car then I'd only be five minutes late.

I saw the car eclipse the hill and start bobbing down the packed blocks of big box store shopping. The bells chimed as if announcing its arrival as my savior but, as it grew closer, one word dashed my hopes – Mason.

There was no way that girl was going to stick around to wait for me. Whatever she had planned wasn't worth forty bucks, or a stranger that tried to flirt with her in a bar. I really debated just heading back to the hotel and calling the whole day a wash. This misfortune was enough to put me off from my other plans of taking in the path to the Golden Gate Bridge, even with how tempting a suicidal leap off it felt.

I hadn't noticed until the car rolled into the turntable that there were actually two on this return trip. One had disconnected and remained behind, and it was one that I desperately needed. What were the odds of bribing the conductor to flip-flop routes with the car behind him? I doubt the tourists in front of me would care. They most likely were just here for the experience. If I hadn't worked for a passenger railroad and knew how important keeping the time schedule was, I'd think there was a chance. I could only hope that the second car would turn and depart soon. So when the second one rolled up not ten minutes later, I wondered if I really hadn't lost my mind and bribed someone.

The car was filling up fast but I knew, one way or another, I was getting on. It didn't bother me that I had to stand. What did bother me was the short Asian woman behind me with a rather pokey shopping bag. The look she gave me quenched any notion of questioning her as to the contents or asking her to remove it from my side. But when the car hit its first turn and it pressed into my side painfully, I seriously debated chucking the bag out the open side windows. It felt like I was a marble in a tin can bouncing around until we crested at Lombard Street, pausing as the conductor played tour guide for a moment for his attentive crowd. I wanted to scream. Any other time would have been a perfect photo opportunity, but not when there was a girl waiting for me. If only the conductor knew how rare this was for me. And a girl that had turned down guys one after another but was taking a chance on my forty bucks and me.

I could see the Hyde Street turntable up ahead. My eyes scanned pass the conductor, seeing streets filled with vendors hocking art, jewelry, knitted hats and scarves. There's a blonde girl, but her long braid is a disappointing jab. The number of blondes in the vast crowds makes the impossibility of this sink in. There never was a chance.

Defeated, I step off when the car comes to a stop. Fifteen minutes late, but time was never the issue. The issue was me. I had fallen for a pretty face and a chance. She could have let me down easy back in the bar instead of leading me on all the way out here. I headed back into the rather short line to head back downtown.

"Jack!"

Turning, I'm surprised it's the California Dime waving and walking my way. She didn't give up on me? She shouldn't be here. That would mean she'd actually be interested in a guy like me. And no one was interested in me. I should have stepped from the line and headed over, but I just can't believe it.

"I was starting to think you weren't going to show." She moves to hug me, catching me off guard. Somehow I manage to think and get my arms to wrap around her to prevent me from looking like a complete idiot.

The line is left behind as we head along the street towards the wharf. "The line was enormous at Powell. I couldn't believe how many tourists are out today. I had thought twenty minutes was going to be enough."

She laughs and that smile is so beautiful. "It's the summer, Jack. There are always tons of tourists. Plus, there's a lot going on this weekend." Dime doesn't point out that I'm one of those. She stops me as we hit the end of the street and I expect we're taking a right into Fisherman's Wharf but we turn to the left and head along the beach. Dime points out the two catamarans on the waves heading this way.

"The World Cup's going on. Race four and five are today. The US came in two games in the hole due to some technicalities from the last meet." She shrugs. "We've almost tied now but it'll take a miracle to win. Everyone's hoping the Kiwis eat some bad tacos or a line breaks."

I had no idea what she was talking about. Kiwis. The fruit or funky looking bird? But who was I to ask when just nodding and playing dumb seemed to be working out in my favor? Then she asked if I watched the sport. At least I had an excuse, or what I hoped was an excuse. I could blame the hotel and being on vacation for why I missed all the other races. Instead, I just shook my head.

"Well, I asked you out here to go to the chocolate festival but now I know you haven't seen these boats in action. We could sit on the beach and watch it if you want to grab something for lunch. Or we can snag our samples and eat our treasures on the docks." She smiled up at me. "I wouldn't object to ruining my lunch with dessert first."

And suddenly, I wouldn't either. "Yea, sure. Let's see what's at the festival and then watch the race." It seemed like either way, I'd be stuck watching the boats.

Cari smiled and walked beside me up to the large chocolate brown building. "I'm guessing that's the Ghirardelli factory?" She nodded. I wondered if it was actually still a factory or if it fell to consumerism like the Hershey factory back in Pennsylvania, with a rollercoaster ride along a fake production line. "Seems like a lot of booths. I didn't think they had that many flavors." Maybe the festival was just setting us up as guinea pigs.

"It's not all Ghirardelli. Local vendors set up a booth, and it's not all chocolate either. Last year, there was this yummy seaweed popcorn. I bought a bag and I swear it was gone before I made it a block."

Seaweed... popcorn? Nothing about that sounded good, but I couldn't exactly criticize her tastes. After all, I was one of them, and I knew I had to be better than seaweed popcorn.

"Jack, did you bring the money?"

The woman at behind the table seemed to be looking for something in one of the bins. I nodded, thinking I had time. Looks like Cari wasn't having me pay her for her wasted time like some horrible prank. It actually seemed like she had already pre-registered. The woman said some name, but it was too quick to catch her full name. Just Cari. I handed over the couple of bills and got two strips of red tickets back.

"These are your tickets. Just give one to the vendor you'd like to sample." The woman behind the table explained, even though it was rather obvious. This wasn't an arcade and there were no prizes strung up in the tent behind her for any other use of the tickets.

I try not to mumble when I thanked the woman and handed Cari a strip. I figured that, seeing as there were only two in the bin for her that this was more like a date where I was expected to pay. Not that I was complaining. If this really was a date, I'd pay the whole way. It was just the grey area of it not being clear what we were doing here that got to me. Do I hold her hand or wrap my arm around her? Should I ask to split the cost?

"So you planned this entire date pretty fast." It must have been a date. What other reason could there be? There were two strips of tickets in a bin with her name on them. I didn't take her as the type to go overboard at something like this. Although, there looked to be more vendors than tickets on the strips.

She had started for the first booth but stopped and looked back slightly confused. "I've had this planned for a couple of weeks."

Okay, that didn't add up. Not when I ruled out her sampling every vendor. "Well, you didn't know me weeks ago." Unless she was in the bar for a reason. Maybe she was looking for a quick date to get her into the festival. A date-and-dump. "It seemed like you were already signed up."

Cari nodded. "Yea, my brother was going to come with me but something came up at work and he couldn't make it." So I was a date-and-dump. I didn't know if that was better or worse than thinking she was supposed to meet up with another guy. "I figured that this probably wasn't in your tourist guide book, and it's something fun to do."

She headed back towards me. "Do you like wine?"

Wine. In the afternoon. Either Cari was an alcoholic or she was thinking about extending this maybe date into the evening. Like before, I couldn't figure out what her end game was.

"It's okay. I don't drink much. Maybe a glass every now and then when I eat out." The Chinese take-out places definitely didn't stock whites and reds for pairings with Mu Shu Pork or General Tso's Chicken. "Why?" I needed to ask to know with her.

"There's a wine tasting here too. My brother's trying to stay sober, so I didn't get tickets for that." She glanced around and seemed to have spotted something. "Yea, okay. It's up on the Creamery Terrace." Turning back to me, she said, "You covered the chocolate festival. What do you say to a little wine?"

This wasn't sounding like a date-and-dump. It definitely would have sounded like a romantic date if it wasn't the middle of the day, in public, off the piers of the Bay. With that smile, it definitely seemed like she was genuinely interested in me... even if we haven't attempted any real affection yet. Maybe I should try to take her hand while we walked around. A little wine would probably help loosen us both up. Maybe this could turn into something a lot more.

"Sure. Why not?" It's not like I'd get this wine tasting opportunity again.

Maybe it was just my imagination but it didn't seem like Cari liked the idea now. It wasn't like Cari had hoped that I'd shoot her down. She was the one mentioning it, which meant it interested her. Maybe it was how I said it after hearing about her brother and that I jumped at the opportunity to guzzle wine in the middle of the day. She could be thinking I'm an alcohol too instead of just trying to be easy-going. Before I could dig myself out of the hole, she says she better get tickets before they sell out... and I just follow her.

There were rows and rows of different vendors. There was a booth for chocolate vodka next to one with little squares of chocolate covered honeycomb. The whole setup stretched two city blocks long and had different booths running the length in four rows. There must have been over fifty different vendors. Of course there are booths showcasing the new Ghirardelli chocolates, and even the Christmas squares coming out at the end of the year.

Cari walks besides me and explains that if I want to try something that sparks my interest to let her know and she'll tear off a ticket so we can try it. There's nothing I see right away that screams at me to go try it. Although, there is a booth with ice cream and it is a rather warm day.

Cari's the first to want to try something and it's... seaweed?

"You sure about this?" I ask. She already has the ticket ripped off and is handing it over to the vendor for the samples.

She nods. "Yea. They were here last year." She must see how hesitant I am to tried dried up ocean grass. "It tastes better than it sounds. I was surprised too. I heard chocolate seaweed and thought it was coated like fruit or something. But they it's just like a flavoring salt on top of popcorn. I mean, they are using popcorn but it's just cocoa powder and tiny flakes of seaweed."

I take the little cup with the questionable kernels. I can see that it's coated popcorn, but it's green. Green isn't a color that popcorn should be.

"Just try it, Jack. I bet you'll like it." I doubt that. "Do it for me?"

Cari had me between a rock and a hard place with that. I picked up one kernel and reluctantly put it in my mouth. I was not enjoying this and it definitely... wasn't as bad as I thought.

"I'd never eat that again."

"But it wasn't, like, horrible, right?" Cari asks.

I shake my head. Not horrible. It was a weird combination, and at least there was no foul aftertaste. I hand her the rest of my sample and stare, a bit in amazement, as she finishes off the odd thing. And then it's onto the next interesting booth.

We're having so much fun. We're leaving, laughing, and barely give a thought to the remaining strip of tickets in our pockets. It's not until we walk by an A-frame sign for the festival and wine tasting do we realize that we've spent the whole day on only half the fun. Well, the delicious half that we couldn't forget.

"Want to head back and try that wine?" It's hard to talk. I'm so out of breath from laughing.

She falls into my side and my arm automatically drifts around her waist. Cari looks up at me with that adorable smile. If it's bothering her, it doesn't show. "Not really, but I'll go with you."

A great day spent with a great girl at a great festival. Did I need to add wine to try and make it better? The only thing was that she paid for the unused wine tickets. "How about we get some dinner instead?"

I expect her to shoot my suggestion down. Instead she snags the strip of tickets peeking out of my pocket and just takes a step away, smiling. "I'll be right back."

Cari took a moment, looking around, before finding her target. She headed over to a couple that was sitting close on a bench talking. I couldn't hear what they were saying, but the guy was a little animated with his hands when he addressed Cari again. Before I knew it, though, she was walking back over.

"What was that about?" She was smiling like the cat that ate the canary.

"Nothing." She gave a little shrug and started on the way we had been walking again. "They just looked like they'd take free tickets to go have a little romantic thing together."

Holy shit.

I don't know if I was more in awe that she was that generous to give our tastings away to complete strangers or that she just admitted it was a romantic thing to do together and gave what we could have had away. I was pretty sure it was the former. Especially when she glanced over her shoulder and asked where I wanted to go. I had to remind myself that, while this may not have started as a date, I asked her out and we were about to get some delicious tacos... somewhere.

Chapter Three

I was getting pretty good at getting around town. It wasn't too hard once I noticed there were schedules at the front desk of my hotel. Luckily there was someone behind the desk that could tell me which routes to avoid. Buses, cable cars, trolleys, taxis, subway, walking. It was more work to find a way not to get somewhere. Cari had thought I'd get lost without her. Well, maybe it was a bit too soon to call that one. Besides, we were basically meeting at the same spot as the other day – only she told me to take the other cable car line to the end and meet her around Mason Street. It was more centrally located along Fisherman's Wharf.

The cornucopia of different brochures in the hotel lobby prepared me for a rather large tourist trap. I could hear a lot of that a few blocks away as I walked towards the cross-streets she said to meet. Part of me was hoping to beat her there so I could show her how savvy I was with the city transit system; the other part, hoping to see her smiling face waiting for me.

Cari was on the phone, facing away, when I stop to wait for the crossing light. There weren't enough cars that darting across the street would be dangerous. I just wanted to take her in a moment longer. Jean cut-off shorts, rosy pink tee, and a 49ers baseball cap, judging by the colors. Her hair was pulled back and drawn through the hole in the back of the cap. I couldn't hear what she was saying, but I could hear her laughing. Whatever was causing it had brightened my day a bit just by hearing it.

The crossing light blinked to the green walking man. As I neared her, she turned and smiled a bit bigger. "I have to go. Yes. I'll call you later." Cari tucked the cell phone in her back pocket and wrapped her arms around me. "Morning."

"Good morning?" I couldn't help but chuckle a little. I wanted to think that I made her morning a good one. That smile was enough encouragement to make me believe that I did.

"Why are you saying that like a question?" She pulled back a little and narrowed her eyes. "Are you trying to say it's not a good morning being with me? I'll tell you that you can have a jolly ole time by yourself today."

That was a turn that I hadn't seen coming. Did it really come off like that? "Cari, no, that's not it." Oh shit, I was ruining this already. "I was just fishing to see if it was a good morning because we were meeting up. Like, better than another morning."

The corner of her mouth twitched a little before a shit-eating grin took over her face. She played me! She played me and now she was laughing. She was laughing and keeling over. Her hand on my shoulder was the only thing keeping her. I wanted to walk away and let her fall. That was a terrible joke to play. Yet... it wasn't that bad. This girl was hot. She was smart and – most importantly – she wanted to be with me.

"Oh, come on, Jack. You don't need to fish around to know if someone likes you or not." Cari started to get it under control after realizing that I wasn't on the same page. "You're not the type of guy that a girl doesn't fall for."

And what type is that?

I wanted to ask but held my tongue. It was hard to imagine a scenario where that question led to anything good. Maybe this was just the sign for Friendsville, population me. It was obvious that Cari hadn't fallen for me. Sure, yesterday at the chocolate festival had been great but it wasn't like it really changed things between us; at least, not for her. I wanted Cari to be my girl more than anyone I've dated since Ava. There was just something about Cari that destroyed who I thought I was because I wanted to be the man that Cari would be with. And because I wanted to be that person, I had to get us back on track.

"So what was the plan for today? I'm guessing you can tell me now." Meaning I'd ignore it.

Cari nodded and seemed to want to put this behind us too. "Well, no tourist trip is complete without a walk down Fisherman's Wharf. And," she smiled a little, "I want to see you behind bars." Okay, was this girl crazy? Had I misread everything the last two days? "We can pick up tickets for Alcatraz and hop the ferry over to the island. It's scary at night with all the ghost stories. You can go; it's just that I can't go with you."

"Because you're afraid of ghosts?" That was a bit of a revelation. I wouldn't have expected her to believe in something so obviously fake. It was never a ghost. It was the wind or a faint echo or a lapse in your brain where a memory wormed out for a second.

"No," she shook her head, "I just... have this thing later." I could tell she was trying to recover her cool. "I really would hate to find out something happened, like you got ate by a ghost, and I wasn't there to see it." Cari laughed as we headed down the crowded sidewalk. It was good to see that we made it back to a good place. I couldn't help wondering what the thing later was, if there was one.

Cari pointed out some shops as we walked by. There really were no reasons to stop in and pick up any souvenirs. My parents were done with my traveling, and it would just be another knick-knack to collect dust for them. I didn't have any kids, who'd probably love to get stuff, and I had no special someone waiting for me. Ava was it, and there was nothing suitable to leave at her grave. It's just not a market these souvenir shops are exploring – grave decorations. I could just imagine it now – *"You're rotting in the ground; I'm rotting in a cell. With love, Alcatraz"*.

"Ever have In-N-Out?" I couldn't say that I have. She continued after I shook my head. "It's a fast food burger joint, but it's not like those other chains. This place is seriously good and the fries are to die for!"

No, there was nothing worth dying for...

I had to shut that thought down fast before I derailed everything I had going with Cari. It was a warm, sunny day and we were having fun. It could be a date, as far as I am concerned. It was just that Ava crept in and I wasn't ready for her. I wasn't used to being around someone long enough to care how I acted when she crossed my mind. Cari must have noticed because the next thing I knew, her hand slipped into mine.

"Come on, Jack. How about I get ya a shake?" She winked before pulling me inside, barely. The line was all the way to the door. I didn't even get the chance to see if Cari was going to give me that shake as she walked up to the counter to order. Nope. Instead I got to take two steps inside the place with her at my side.

"This place is pretty busy." Never saw any of the other burger joints like this, except maybe for ten minutes at peak lunch time.

She laughed. "It's pretty much like this all day, but it's so worth it." Cari smiled up at me. "If you don't like it, you can have a freebie to make me suffer through anything to pay you back."

Well that opened up a lot of opportunities. Of course, she was probably thinking food-related. But why couldn't I get a kiss out of it or another date? Yesterday was great, but this morning already was a little rocky. It didn't feel quite like a sure thing anymore. I was pretty sure that I wasn't ready for this thing between us to end as *"just friends"*. There's no way that I wouldn't be trying, and hoping, that she'd be with me. I think it would hurt more to walk away from her and test the waters again in this city, or anywhere. I'd be drawn to every blonde bob of hair from the corner of my eye, real or imaginary. I didn't want to be nursing a break-up when I came here to get away from the biggest one in my life, and the only one I had no control over.

"Jack." She was staring up at me a little accusatory. "Where'd you go just now? I was talking to you and you just had this glazed over look."

"I was right here." Okay, so maybe I was still a little guarded. I hadn't meant to mentally drift off. I didn't want to end up ruining the time we had together; however, I realized that the words were slipping out of my mouth again without a filter and pushing us closer to another rift. "I was just thinking about us."

Shit. That wasn't the right thing to say. There really wasn't an "us". Labels were so far away right now that I could almost see the gears in her mind telling her to run. It was one thing when a girl labeled a relationship – and completely socially acceptable – but it was entirely something else when the guy uttered those words first. With Ava and I, it was more that our friends called us a couple and we just went with it until we couldn't remember a time when we weren't an actually together. It blurred perfectly into a life together.

Shit. I did it again. When I risked a glance over at her, Cari seemed fine. She was just looking ahead and I realized that we were next in line to order. Had she said something and I completely missed it? Had she asked me to leave and was pretending that I didn't exist? I was sure that I had screwed this up and had no idea I was doing it.

Cari ordered, getting an extra side of fries, and turned to me. Okay, so nothing seemed to have happened. Maybe she hadn't caught me this time. I just asked the guy at the register to give me what she was having. I pulled out my wallet. Date or not, I was paying. Out of the corner of my eye, I could see Cari was reaching for her bag.

"I got this. My treat." I smiled and was relieved that she beamed up at me.

"Thanks, Jack. I'll go grab us a seat. Mind sitting out back in the courtyard?" I shook my head and watched her grab her drink cup. I couldn't take my eyes off her as she filled the cup to the brim with Cherry Fanta and walked out the side door. I'm not sure how, but I hadn't screwed this up... yet. Maybe I wasn't such a hopeless cause.

The thing about In-N-Out Burger was that, for having an enormous line, the food showed up fast, correct, and smelled delicious. I wanted to devour the whole tray and forget about letting Cari grab a bite... then end up alone and beat myself up for always deflecting and pushing people away.

"I don't know how, but they messed up our order." I pulled the chair out with my foot and sat down across from Cari once I made it outside. It looked like she was about to say something and I didn't want to risk her taking it seriously, again. "Yea, your whole order is just missing... 'cos this is all mine."

Her face changed from concern to disbelief. "You jerk!" She smacked my arm playfully. "You can't mess with me about my fries like that." Cari snatched one off the tray and popped it into her mouth before I could even think of a witty comeback to that. There was a moment of silence between us before we both busted out laughing.

"So just the fries?" I teased. She shook her head, still laughing. I could really get used to that sweet noise.

Cari didn't pretend around me either. She took a bite of her burger and it was a real bite. There weren't salads on the menu, but I don't think she would have ordered one just to feint being dainty for me. And she didn't pretend not to enjoy that burger. Those noises were sweet, but for a whole other reason.

"Do you two wanna to get a room?"

Cari blushed and I couldn't help chuckling. It was like I had caught her in the worst possible way. "It's just... good," she tried to defend with a mouthful.

Not pretending one minute.

The burgers looked worth it though. They weren't wrapped up in some waxed paper or jammed in a box. They were topped and lovingly embraced in a paper wrap and looked picture-perfect. For once, something on the menu or billboard looked like what was about to go in my mouth. And the smells were just as divine.

"Well, are you going to eat that?" Cari teased. She pretended like she was waiting to snatch it away.

I had to grab it now, and not just for show. There was a time to appreciate something and a time to act. "I was just admiring this masterpiece." She sighed as if it was the greatest disappointment in the world. "It looks almost too good to eat."

"Then let me eat it if you're too upset to destroy art." Obviously a taunt, but not one I was buying. I made a slight show by taking a bite, and even tossed in some moans for extra measure.

Cari rolled her eyes. "You're unbelievable." As punishment, she stole one of the fries on my tray. "But seriously, what do you think?"

"So a little moaning isn't a good sign?" Oh, wow. This was turning south fast. Hopefully it was only in my mind; yet, part of my mind hinged on her reply and threated to just lose it. Would a few sweet noises out of her nothing but a fake compliment? Was the bar set higher at making her scream my name?

She said nothing and took another bite out of her burger. Had she caught on? I was growing more obvious with my attraction the longer I was around her. Maybe Cari just took it as a sarcastic comment that didn't warrant a response. Either way her silence was killing me. I wanted to point it out so many times, but how? If she wasn't into me or choosing to dismiss it, then I would drive her away and make things awkward between us. Cari was the shining light on this trip. If she caught on and was drawing it out until I cracked, did I really want to rush into that discussion? There was still a chance that I could make a fool out of myself.

"You got a lot on your mind, huh?" Glancing up, those two blue orbs watched me. It was almost like the wide-eyed look children get in front of a candy store. And it scared the hell out of me; because, right now, it was like Cari was seeing me – actually seeing me – and I had no clue how she would take that. She must know that I have baggage. She must know what a coward I am to be running from the past. Even if it was all in my mind, it was a scary responsibility.

"Naw, just really enjoying this burger. You were right. This place is pretty awesome." At least it was the truth. Although twisted to cover up the answer she wanted, it was honest. The burger was pretty awesome. "You wouldn't by chance know an awesome place for dessert around here too?"

Cari laughed and shook her head. "I know this pretty awesome ice cream place but it's not really close by."

She had finished her fries by the time I was through with my piece of art and half my fries. I knew she wouldn't ask or try to steal the fries, but I split them with her. It wasn't this Tramp's spaghetti dinner with my Lady, but it definitely was a moment. I just had to hope she felt something too.

I had thought that I'd be able to pay for this adventure. Turned out Cari already had tickets. I wasn't sure if she had them laying around or if she picked them up last night. I do know that I was a little amazed at how planned out everything was. She, like so many others out here, were just so laid back and carefree. I guess I fell under the assumption that she couldn't possibly have things in order because of it. At the same time, it made me envious that people out here were so carefree and still had things handled.

"So, seeing me behind bars... Are you still planning to lock me up?" Staring at the ticket while we waited for the line to move for the ferry, I realized how off the mark I had been when I took it the wrong way earlier. There had been exactly three things that I knew about San Francisco before I got here – cable cars, Golden Gate Bridge, and Alcatraz – and only one of them really had bars. It wasn't even like I had assumed it was some off-the-cuff comment about how we met in the moments before she mentioned the prison.

Her hand slipped into mine. "Guess that depends on you and if you behave. I mean, you did pull that stunt and try to steal my In-N-Out."

She stepped up to the security check and handed over her ticket. It didn't take long for the guard to check her bag, but it did give me a couple minutes to appreciate the girl that was spending her day with me... and those tanned legs. God, what I'd give to have those wrapped around me. Just the thought was enough to almost distract me from my turn at being checked, and got me dangerously close to being suspected of carrying a concealed weapon – in my pants.

We climbed on the ferry and I found Cari's hand back in mine. I couldn't complain, especially when a moment later she was in my arms. Her chest flush up against mine and her eyes staring deep. A light rosy blush started in her cheeks and spread until that cute little nose turned red.

"I, uh..." Cari stammered. Was it because we ended up so close? She hadn't moved away. That had to be a good thing. The timing could have been better. I'd rather we weren't surrounded by a bunch of tourists, but that wasn't enough to just give up. I started to lean in for a kiss when she apologized. "I'm sorry. I can't really walk on boats. Poor balance."

And just like that, the wind was knocked from my sails. The ferry rocked a little against the dock and just drove home how stupid I was. Why hadn't that been my first thought? It wasn't like Cari had ever admitted to our days together as dates. And I almost kissed her! I wanted to kiss her so bad – and it was just the damn boat.

"Well, then let's find a place to sit. Don't want you falling into anyone else." I wish the tone of my words wasn't so disappointed. No matter how I tried to perk up my thoughts, it was nothing but a letdown. Part of me was disappointed that I didn't just go for it. The other was angry at the boat. But all of it was still thinking about Cari. Her hand in mine. How she sat close on the bench by one of the ferry's windows.

"Any motion sickness I should look out for? I'm sure I can find a paper bag before we leave the dock." I was less concerned about vomit and more needing a distraction from having her in my arms. Cari felt too good.

She shook her head. "You'd think a little wave wouldn't knock me over. Not when I get on stage and –" The ship rocked more, pressing her up against my side, as it pushed off from the dock. It had ended her train of thought while killing me to have her so close again. She didn't move away and I spent the whole trip out to The Rock debating what that meant – *if* it meant anything. And what had she been trying to say about a stage and her up on one?

Getting off the ship was the same thing. Her hand slipped into mine, as if nothing happened. Did she know the kind of feelings she stirred up in me? Knowing that Cari meant nothing by it, and still kept doing it, was a slap in the face. Yet, I couldn't bring myself to ask her to stop. It was a delusion that I wanted to keep going. Maybe pretending to be with a girl like her might finally get me over Ava.

"Do you want to hit the gift shop now or start at the top?"

Cari smiled up at me. The baseball cap shadowed half her face but those eyes still shone too brightly my way. I didn't want her to affect me anymore, but it was like that never was an option. My heart would willingly break and bleed for just a smile.

"Why don't we start up top? We won't have to hike up with all the bags and it would probably be better to get it out of the way while we still feel up to it."

It was hard to still want to see this prison after glancing up the steep path. It hadn't looked like it back at the dock, but it looked like you had to hike up a mountain. It definitely wasn't something I wanted to wait and anticipate doing later. At least if we got it out of the way now, I could just roll my way back down to the ferry later.

A honk from behind us had us jumping out of the way just as we started up the steep incline. A golf cart trolley zoomed by, carrying tourists up the hill.

"You have to be kidding me." The shuttle was up and disappearing around the bend before we even got back on the road. "We could have gotten a ride up?"

Cari glanced my way and shrugged. Guess I couldn't put blame on her either way. I wanted to just to justify my mislaid feelings from earlier but – I noticed now – she hadn't taken my hand on the walk. On the ferry, I was a crutch. The other times had to simply be a fluke.

Neither of us said anything as we headed to the top of The Rock, walking pass a couple broken buildings and the morgue. It took the park rangers at the prison entrance to get her to say a word or even look at me. And then it was just to answer their question of which language, out of the dozen choices, we needed. English.

A man in a weathered green uniform and brimmed hat handed me what looked like a television remote and a set of headphones. He broke it down for me as if I was a child and got me set on where to start the self-guided tour and how to wear the controller so it didn't get damaged. Another ranger helped Cari behind me; I could hear the same spiel. I wasn't going to start without her and I wanted things to somehow find a way back to how they were before. At least I could accept it now for what it was, and avoid this awkwardness between us.

With how the tour was set up and with the already forming crowd, Cari would have to walk beside me. We stopped just on the perimeter of the crowd as the headset started in with sounds of Alcatraz and welcoming us to the most famous prison. The crowd moved us along as the monologue started in about the amenities of the cells in this block and where work detail were occasionally allowed to go. When the mass got to the end of the row, it merged with one there and Cari was no longer beside me. I had no clue where she went. I couldn't see her or her hat. I was getting worried that something happened to her – how was I ever going to find her? – when I felt something against my hand. Cari was pushed into me by a pushy tourist, but it had been her hand that found me first.

"You okay?" I mouthed, knowing she couldn't hear me through the headphones. She nodded.

After how the walk up went, I had expected her hand to disappear the moment the crowds thinned. But it didn't. Hers remained in mine as we walked through the library and dining room and where the great prison fight broke out. We listened to how the escapees actually made it out and stared up at the large wall, imagining how they scaled the inside, together. It wasn't until solitary that her warmth disappeared.

"Okay, behind the bars." I glanced in at the dark, dank cell and shook my head. I was normally a very trusting person, but this was a little too much. "Jack, they have the locks off. Come on, it's just a photo opp."

She pulled out her cell phone, but that hardly set me at ease. A better photo would be of me stuck inside the cell. That one would probably get the most likes on social media. Hell, Cari could probably sell me as a souvenir. It was just that this cell felt permanent and cold while she was free out in the muted sunshine freedom.

"Oh, here, let me take that. Why don't you get in the photo with your fella?" A short greying woman waddled over with her fanny pack. I had expected Cari to say something – either on the front of being locked in a cell as well or that the woman just claimed we were together. Instead, she just smiled and handed over her phone. Cari pulled me behind the bars and wrapped her arm around my back at the waist.

"Baby," she giggled. Cari definitely was enjoying this.

"Fella, get a little closer to the lady." I could blame this lady. Yes, there would be an excuse for stepping over the line. I moved closer and pulled Cari against me. "Okay, now smile. Three... two... one... Perfect!" Instead of smiling, I kissed her cheek.

Cari headed around to check out the photo, her smile growing bigger. Obviously it was a good one. Before I could get out to take a peek, she had the phone back in her pocket. Guess maybe later then. Although it struck me odd that she didn't offer to show me. Maybe I looked terrible. Maybe it was better that I didn't see it. Or maybe she realized that things between us could change.

Her hand slipped into mine while she busied herself with the audio set for the next tour location. It was like that for the rest of the tour. Her hand stayed in mine and I sure as hell wasn't going to question it.

"So, do you want to hit the gift shop? You know, stock up on all those knickknacks." She giggled.

I had the urge to roll my eyes. I knew that she wasn't completely taking a trip through the gift shop seriously. "Yea, let's see what they got." It was nice to throw her off her game a little. Although Cari quickly recovered, I could still see a bit of sass on her face. She was dying to say something else.

"So what about you? Are you going to pick something up to remember your amazing time here?" I wondered if this was her first time here. She could have lived here but never played tourist before. Then again, I had practically lived in Philly and never saw the Liberty Bell. I got a tour of the courts, but never the few blocks over to see the chunk of metal.

"I don't know." Cari seemed to think for a moment as we strolled into the shop area. She glanced around. "I don't really need anything and I can't really use a sweatshirt."

Oh, those looked nice. Orange sweatshirts with stripes and an inmate tag from Alcatraz stamped across the front hung on the wall in rows. Just too embarrassing to wear in public.

"You should try one on anyways, Cari. I can just take your picture." And I could get a chance to see the photos from before that were somewhere on her phone. She rolled her eyes and I thought she was going to give in, but she just walked away to look at postcards.

We ended up walking out with nothing but each other. Her hand had found its way back into mine before we hit the ferry, but her mind seemed to be somewhere else. The sound of waves against the boat was the only sound to interrupt the silence. Then it was the cling clang of the cable cars at the Hyde Street turntable. I wondered if I had done something wrong to have caused this distance.

"Want me to grab you a ticket before we get on?" I had wised up and got a pass. I knew that – not entirely because of Cari – that I'd be riding the cable cars more than once. They just brought out that excitement of a carnival ride and, in a way, that was almost appropriate to love them and have a ridiculous grin plastered on your face the whole trip.

Cari's hand dropped out of mine. "No, I'm actually not heading back downtown. I'm meeting up with some friends, but thanks for offering." She smiled, but it seemed strained.

I noticed there was no invitation there. I knew that I shouldn't be waiting for one. We hadn't known each other that long, really, and Cari probably felt like a tour guide. She probably wanted some time away from me.

"No problem." I started to walk towards the boarding line. No point in letting her see the disappointment.

"Jack." I paused and glanced over my shoulder. What could she want? "Do you run?"

Run? Can't say that I do. The only time was when a crazy man with a gun was chasing me. But Cari looked like she did and there had to be a reason that she asked. Hopefully she had thought of a way to see each other again, because I couldn't and I didn't want this to be the last I saw of her.

I shrugged. "What did you have in mind?" Yea, that was an easy way around it. It gave me time to think something up. Because, let's face it, running wasn't something I was exactly thrilled about.

"Well, I go for a run every morning. Do you want to come with?" She fidgeted a little while I mulled it over. It would be an excuse to see her. Hell, maybe I could even impress her. I nodded and her smile grew a little. "Okay, I'll just head over to your hotel in the morning and we'll go from there. Guess I'll see you in the morning." Cari waved before heading off.

Chapter Four

"I can't believe that you're serious." I groan as I bent over to tie my running shoes. Why I had I thought to pack comfortably? If I hadn't then maybe I could have gotten out of running with Cari today. Who am I kidding? She'd have just told me to head to one of the stores and stop being a wuss. That and I'd lose time to hang out with her. It really feels like there might be something with her, a connection or something. I just know that she makes me feel a whole lot happier when she's around.

"Jack, if you don't get your ass down here in five minutes then I'm switching our path to include all the lovely hills you love so much."

Wise ass.

Cari knew how much walking uphill, both ways, to get anywhere in this city killed me. At least I don't have to watch her laugh at me... just hear it. I hoped that I'm dressed enough to look like I've at least attempted to run before. I hope she's not decked out in runner clothes – sports bra and tight running pants. Then again, I really hope Cari is decked out in runner clothes.

"I can hear you laughing, you know." It just gets her to laugh even more. I chuckle as I roll my eyes. "I'm hanging up now. See you in a sec'." I hung up the room phone and headed down to the lobby.

Whatever route she's planned out, I doubt it's going to be easy for me; so, I might as well take every luxury that I can. I step off the elevator into the lobby and see her leaning against the front desk, reading the wine tasting pamphlet. And, hell, this is going to be a rough run. She's wearing tight black running shorts and a tie-dye colored sport cami. If my feet don't trip me up, the partial in my pants problem would. And if she was running in front of me? I was going to be a goner. I knew she had a nice body but, hell, it was so much better in those clothes. I can only imagine how she'd look laid out completely –

"Come on lazy bones. Stop slacking!" She laughs and playfully punches my arm when she catches me staring at her. "I could have got a couple miles in by the time it's taken you to get down here. I was starting to think you were bailing," she teases.

She has to know that wasn't the case. We've spent almost every day together since the bar. Cari makes me do a couple stretches before we head out of the hotel. I go along with her because I have no idea how running works. The only time I had to run was when that crazy cop was trying to shoot me, after all.

"You caught me," I laugh, "I was going to hide in my room and pig out on all the chocolate from the festival."

"You're horrible!" She shakes her head and I can see her smile growing bigger. As much as I've probably disrupted her normal schedule, she's enjoying it. I really hope that she's loving being together as much as I am.

Cari heads off Sutter and head up Kearny for a few blocks. I see ahead with what looks like a white toothpaste cap on top a mountain.

"Cari?" I ask wearily, wondering if she was really changing the route to kill me. She just laughs and bumps my elbow as we turn just a few blocks shy of the incline and take Columbus Avenue. It's such a relief that she's not trying to kill me... at least not yet.

"Cutting through the hills," she breathes out without breaking the mild pace she's set for us. "Hit the Bay Trail. Five miles to the bridge."

Shit.

Maybe I should have told her that by little running experience, I meant none. Unless she had a gun tucked somewhere in those fitting clothes, there was no way I was going to make it. And thinking of a gun, more exactly places she could be have one concealed, definitely was a terrible distraction.

It's hard just to keep breathing and play it cool, so I can't argue that plan. Nothing is familiar, so I can't even suggest an alternate route. It's not until we hit Beach Street that I see the cable car turntable and know where I am. I can't believe we're ran that far already and I'm still alive. Unfortunately, I remember seeing how far that bridge was from here the few times I've been in this part of town.

"Cari... stop... please." They all come out as gasps, but it's more of a miracle that they were words at all. She must have heard me, even though she was a couple feet ahead, and she slowed to a light jog until there was a free bench. I don't give her a second to sit. I collapse on it, greedily taking every inch to bring much needed relief to my lower limbs.

She's chuckling as my body rocks a little. It takes a moment to realize that she's working my muscles. "You're all tense. Jack, you should have told me. You'll kill yourself running like that."

I groan as I feel her thumbs dig in and work out the tension of my calves. "You should have told me we were running all the way to China." At least between her hands and the cool ocean breeze, I'm not completely miserable. As if I'm her personal clown, she's laughing. Not that I truly care. I'm really starting to fall hard over that laugh. It almost makes all the pain worth it.

"How bad of a tourist would I be if I never got to that bridge?" I have a feeling that I know the answer, but I'm wondering the reasoning Cari would give me.

She moves to sit at the end of the bench and takes my legs onto her lap to keep working my muscles. "A horrible one, seeing as that was the like the only thing you could tell me about the city in the bar." I can tell Cari's thinking about how we met. Probably how awkwardly strange I was, and hopefully how much better I am now. "I think I would be a bad tour guide if I didn't get you there."

"You know you're more than that."

I'm not sure if I really meant that to come out. Every other time I moved to take that next step, or even to let a girl know that I wanted more, they panicked. And lying like this, she has the benefit to hide her face as she focuses on my abused legs. I don't know where her head is at with us, or even if she thinks that there could be an "us". And I want that us. It's just that her silence is killing me because the longer that it goes on the more I know she's talking herself out everything between us this week. I want to fight for her to see what we are, what we could be. Unlike the other girls, I am fighting the hardest for Cari.

"What if I don't want to be?"

The words gut me when she finally speaks. I had jumped too soon and scared her off. I could almost see the walls going up and I had to say the only thing I could. "Then you'll just be what you want."

She nods slowly before getting up. "Come on." She puts my feet on the ground and tries to pull me up to sit. "We have a few more miles to clock. I want to get you to that bridge," she adds with a smile.

Tour guide.

The moment I try to stand, my legs feel like buckling. They're feeling better, don't get me wrong, but any healing Cari did seemed void after what she said. I know that I'm not going to be able to run the rest of the way, and I know there'd still be the same miles waiting for me on the way back to my hotel.

"Cari, I think I'm just going to call it a day. I'm not going to be able to make it and I don't want to slow you down on your run. I'm just going to head back to the hotel and-"

"Jack, stop... please," she cuts me off. "I didn't say we were going to run. Just... walk with me?"

What is it about the way she asked that is making me want to bend over backwards for her? I should tell her no and head back to my room. I only have a couple days left here and maybe she realized our time was ending. As much as I hate how temporary this all could be, maybe it's best if it is. I'll have classes when I get back and I still have to move into campus housing before my parents break into my apartment and move me home with them.

"Okay," I concede. I know running is not an option, but so is leaving her. I'm not ready for that. I can tell by how far off the orange bridge looks that this is going to be a long walk. I'm not sure if this is going to be more awkward than if I just left or not.

"You're not really a runner." It wasn't quite a question. "So why'd you agree to come this morning?"

Sighing, I know her reaction isn't going to be good. She has to know that already when I pointed out that she was more than a tour guide to me. There just didn't seem to be any way to get her to accept that. Maybe I could convince her this time. If not, then it was never going to happen.

"I've spent almost every day here with you, Cari, and I didn't want to miss being with you. I came here to get away. Meeting you, you make me want to stay. And I figured it was going to be a mile or two run. I figured that I could fake it long enough to get you to like me."

Did she just blush?

"Come on, Jack. Don't you have someone back home? Someone like you can't stay single for long." She tucked a stray strand of hair behind her ear and must have realized how that sounded. "I mean, you're like the dream guy. There's no way you're living the single life."

And I'm lying to her by being here? I had said I was getting away from stuff and she assumed now that it meant a girl. I hated that she humored that horrible thought of me, but I couldn't hold it against her. She was so beautiful and great that I could be asking her too if she was seeing me on the side.

"I'm a hundred percent single. I'm too damaged for any girl to want me." The sad truth had slipped out and I can see her look from the corner of my eye. Unlike other times, it almost feels okay to bring up Ava. "My fiancée was murdered a few years ago and I guess I struggled more to get over her death than I thought. I'm pretty sure I've tried to find the furthest place I can get from her, but she's always there. Coming here was just another try to escape her... and my parents. They think I can't handle life anymore and want me to move in with them so they can watch me. I think one of those talk shows my mom watches has her thinking I'm suicidal."

Her hand on my arm stops me and I realize that I was wrong. The look she gave me wasn't of doubt. It had been more of understanding. "Look, Cari, I didn't tell you that to get your pity. I... it just came out. I never talk about Ava."

"I get it, but she sounds like she was a big part of you and you want to forget her."

"Cari, you don't understand. I have to forget that life because I'll never have it. Every time I think about her, I remember all the times I failed her. Hell, I should have been there when she died. And it wasn't just her that I lost. Ava was pregnant. I lost my fiancé and my..." Arms wrap around me. The single most reaction to my loss had always been a hug, but it felt different this time.

"You love them, Jack. You'll never escape because you will never stop loving them. And in no way does that make you damaged or undesirable. Not. In. The. Least." She moved back a little to look up at me. "You just have a big heart that you're scared to let people see, and I don't think there's a single part of you that you should hide."

I did still love them. A tear streaked down my face, but it was the gentle touch brushing them away that caught me. I had been wrong again with that look. There was never any pity in her eyes. Cari got me, somehow. She understood and accepted me, accepted all of me... and that pain inside didn't feel so great anymore.

"Can I take you somewhere?" Her voice was quiet. There was no reason to refuse. I alright committed myself to being with her today and now, with these thoughts, I really shouldn't be alone in a hotel room, depressed.

She takes my silence as a yes and starts to head back towards the city. She keeps glancing my way to make sure I haven't bolted. Maybe I should. I shared something so personal that I shouldn't have, and it was also the thing that drove off the other girls I tried to date. There's just something about Cari and I can tell it's more than looks drawing me to her. Even knowing her now, there's still something else about her that I can't get out of my head.

I'm so lost in my head that I don't notice the odd triangle-shaped door. It gives her a laugh when I slam to a complete stop and just stare at what looks like an upside down ice cream cone that fell on the ground. Even the paint job on the building gave that illusion... a very delicious illusion. I just can't understand why this is the place she took me. Who needed to ask someone if they wanted to get ice cream?

She holds the door open for me, and then runs into my back when I stop just inside the door. I froze, seeing the neon graffiti of ice cream cult art with the retro feel of the ice cream shop. Laughing, she pushes me in before taking my hand and leading me to the end where there are two fire engine red stools.

"Never had ice cream before, Jack?" She teases and takes a twirl around her seat while waiting for me to snap out of it.

Ice cream, yes. Been in a place like this, no. I just couldn't get the image of a gang member spray painting a scoop of ice cream with sprinkles on the side of some building. You can't be gangster and draw neon sprinkles on what looks like a scoop of blue moon ice cream. Uh huh.

"What is this place?"

Cari stops spinning to beam a smile my way. "It's Greg's Sock Hop."

Oh, yea, that clearly was the only explanation.

"It used to be Greg's Scoop, but my group always came here after our shows and someone started teasing him that it looked like a sock hop going down."

She shrugs. Somewhere along our walk here, she's gotten cryptic. It has me thinking that maybe it's going to be less about my past and more about being distracted by her.

"Cari, I have no idea what you're talking about and I doubt it's an after effect of your recent murder attempt." I try to joke hoping to pick us, well, pick me back up. "You know that I probably have no clue what a sock hop is and now I want to hear about this group of yours."

I lean forward a bit. She's not going to weasel out of this, not that she wants to. Cari purposely was vague and left herself open. The smile she struggles to hide is proof of that.

Cari leans in and I try not to think about how close her face is to mine right now. This is the closest she's come to me and I don't want to risk scaring her off by pointing it out. "Well, a sock hop is kind of like a school dance, but back in the 50s. Think like poodle skirts, leather jackets and big hair... well, like Grease. You've seen those movies, right?"

I nod and she continues. "Well, about five years back, I was in a dance group. We did theme stuff. Monday was monster, so it was like a huge Halloween-fest. Tuesday was tangos and just sexy dresses... and Friday was flashback. We just kind of got stuck in the 50s and, after our shows, Greg's was the only place nearby that was still open. So we'd stop in for dessert before heading home, and most of us were still in our costumes. It kind of drew a crowd here, so Greg changed the name. We haven't done that for a while. Our group leader was in the navy and got reassigned out East, so we voted on some new routines."

"Hello, jive turkeys, I'm Shimmy Sam and I'll be your waiter. You dig? Can I get you two love birds anything?"

Shit. One, I hadn't looked at the menu at all. And two, he thinks we're a couple. He called us out as a couple. I glance back to Cari and there's no reaction as she smiles up at the unfortunate teen that has to call himself Shimmy Sam. Was she okay with that? Was I the only one panicking? Why the hell was I panicking? That's what I wanted with her. It's been almost a week, so it's hardly too soon.

"And you, cool cat?"

Two sets of eyes are on me. Shit. I should have been paying attention. But where was the menu? It wasn't up on the wall over the ice cream bar, and Cari probably had it memorized. This was getting worse by the second and the illusion I could keep it together for five minutes was shattering.

"Um, menu?"

The guy didn't seem fazed. Okay, so maybe it wasn't just me that struggled with this. Maybe it was some kind of thing where you just toss out a flavor and they make it. That bar was long. It probably housed at least forty flavors, not that I could name more than twelve.

Cari helps me out when she points to the space in front of me. I'll be damned. Right under the clear plastic tablecloth was a menu... and it was quite large. There were flavors and shakes and sundaes and specialties that made my head hurt just imagining what a Surfin' Spaghetti Man would look like, let alone how it would taste.

"Rockin' Robin is one of my favorites. Chocolate ice cream with a scoop of strawberry and fresh berries. It taste just like you're dipped them in a chocolate fountain. But if you get that, I'm making you share with me."

With that smile? I'd give her the whole thing. But the idea of sharing with her made this seem more like a date than I was sure it was. We were just supposed to go for a run today, but it turned into this and having the waiter pegging us as a couple. All the while, Cari sat unfazed. Maybe it really was a date.

Had the Californian dime fallen for a nickel? I was going to have to see just how far she fallen. Could she really be mine?

"I'll have to get the Rockin' Robin then." I give her a wink and, holy hell, she blushed. Okay, so this was more than just two strangers out together. Cari wasn't the type to be embarrassed by something like that, and she had taken the waiter's comments in stride. The guy didn't miss a beat and headed off to give us some privacy now that he took our orders.

"So..."

I smile and watch as she tries to avoid eye contact. "So." There's no way I'm going to let her off the hook. There's something on her mind and she's trying to volunteer me to change the subject; which, there's no way I'm doing that.

Cari squirms a little before she comes out and asks. "Ever seen a burlesque show?"

I damn near fall off the chair. Burlesque? Out of all the things she could have asked me that was not one of them. I expected something about the fact we were being pegged as a couple or what we were doing, as in with each other, or any of the other equally hard and awkward questions a typical person would want to know. Not that I'd list Cari as typical anything.

"I can't say that I ever have. Why do you ask?" Oh, shit. Is she trying to figure out why kind of guy I am? Or maybe this was some part of the plans tomorrow to take in a show? Did I want to see a strip tease with her? No. Well, at least not with her. Of her was a completely different matter. But wait, those shows were mainly female performers. Was this the nail in the coffin that Cari was a lesbian? Oh, god, I hope that wasn't true. The least she could be was bi-sexual. At least I'd have a chance then and...

"That's what my group does now. We have a show Monday night. I could get you a ticket if you want to come."

This girl had to stop throwing me for a loop. Either that or I should take up residency on the floor right now. Basically, she was asking if I'd come and watch her strip. It was hard enough to see her in those tight running clothes. Seeing her up on a stage bearing it all was going to kill me. Then there was the fact that I wouldn't be the only one ogling her. Right away, I wanted to tell her that there was no way in hell she was doing that. Not as long as she was my... Okay, so I really didn't have any say in her life and this was something she had been doing for a while. It wasn't like there weren't hundreds of guys, possibly, walking around with a mental image of her that I could never force them to erase.

"Huh... I guess I've never had a girl invite me to watch her get naked on stage in front of a bunch of people before. I... I'm not sure what I'm supposed to say."

"Oh, no! Jack," her hand's on mine again and it dissolves everything we just talked about, "burlesque isn't stripping. Well, it is but we don't go nude. The women have on pasties and thongs, and the men just thongs."

Men. In. Thongs.

That visual was enough to kill whatever reaction I got from picturing Cari naked. I definitely never wanted to see that. "Oh, that's tempting. I mean, men in thongs... always wanted to see that. I think I'm going to have to pass." That and I would be back in Pennsylvania come Monday. I had to sign the lease on my new place and get my stuff moved in before classes started up.

"I guess that I should have left that for a surprise."

Shit. Cari thinks that I turned her down for that. Didn't she realize by now that I'd sport a thong if it meant something to her – not that I was going to offer that up willingly. Before I could say anything to correct that silly little head of hers, the waiter was back with two heaping bowls.

"What the hell is that?" I couldn't take my eyes off it.

Cari laughed. Obviously this wasn't anything unusual. But how could something overflowing what looked to be a fishbowl and heaped a mile high be normal? Let alone, how was I going to finish that? It was a good thing that she offered to split mine.

"Still thinking about stealing half of this?"

"Half?" She laughed. "I don't think I agreed to half." Well, not exactly half but there was definitely going to be some sharing involved.

"Why did you let me order my own if you knew neither of us could possibly fit all this in our gut? I would have been fine with almost anything."

Why was she blushing again? That was twice in, like, ten minutes. "Well, maybe you can't put it away but I definitely can, and have, cleaned out a bowl here before. Besides, I didn't think you'd want to make things awkward by sharing?"

Maybe I was oblivious. "Why would that make things awkward?"

"You know, it would be more like a date…"

"Why would that be awkward for me? I like you, Cari. A lot." Might as well clear that up, again. But how could she not realize that? "I thought you'd be the one feeling awkward after Slappy Sam called us a couple."

"Slappy Sam?" It got a laugh out of her. "First, it's Shimmy Sam; and second, I thought you just saw me as a friend. I mean, it's been almost a week and you haven't so much as made a move. Until you turned me down about the guys in thongs, I thought you might be a little…"

"What? No." I guess choosing to come to such an iconic spot for those human rights could blur the line. "I wasn't sure you were single at first and that you were even interested in me. I thought if I made you hang out with me every day that something might change or I'd realize how crappy we'd be as a couple."

"Well, I didn't expect you to be a swinging single either."

"Is that a stab at Slappy Sam?"

She can't wipe off that smile now that I got her going. "Shimmy Sam."

"Shimmy... Slappy... I'm not calling him Sexy."

"Calling who sexy, you cool cat?" That did it. Cari busted out in a side-splitting laugh that landed her hunched over the table. Our waiter had the silent skills of a ninja.

"My sexy kitty cat, here?" It was a struggle not only to say those words, but also to keep from laughing. "A cool cat gots to have a sexy kitty, right?"

The guy nodded. "Totally, dude." And just like he came, he was gone.

"Did that just happen?" Cari sounded out of breath, but somehow sexy at the same time. Yea, my sexy kitty cat.

I nod. "I think he bought it. That or he agrees with me and I might need to rough him up a bit for looking at my woman." The look on Cari's face means that she caught that last part. I hadn't meant to call her mine, at least not out loud to her face. Although, it doesn't seem to be an issue anymore.

"So you're a dancer, or do you prefer an entertainer?"

Cari reaches over and snatches up a scoop with one of my berries littering the heap of the melting wonder. "Definitely entertainer. If you came to my show you'd see. But that's not my real job." She slowly savored that spoonful and I'd be damned if I didn't with I was that scoop. "I work at a Starbucks downtown. It's horrible with how busy it gets in the mornings, but I have a couple friends that work there. After the rush, we usually make a game out of it by timing each other or making codenames for the drinks. It's not too bad."

She tries to steal another bite but when my spoon gets close to hers, Cari pull back, thinking I challenged her to a duel. I was only planning on stealing a taste of hers and, wow, did she have good taste.

"So, that's me. What about you, Mr. Swipey Hands?"

I couldn't help chuckle at my new name. "Swipey Hands? You know, that means I'll have to come up with something for you," I tease. I'm partial to My Sexy Kitty Cat and it seems like she is too when she reminds me that I already gave her one.

"Now, come on, tell me what you do! I want to know the real Jack." She's waving her spoon at me. I know it's supposed to come off as threatening, but it's not. Cari's a little too comical with her antics for her to ever be that.

"Okay," I chuckle. I know that I can't evade the question and I really don't want to with her. "I'm going back to school and studying photography. I figured it would be fun and my friends at work always said my photos were pretty good. After what happened with Ava, I figured it was better than nothing." She wants to ask; I know she does. I've brought up Ava again, right after laying claim to her. Hell, we were here because of Ava. And she's struggling with how she wants to broach it. I don't let her sweat it.

"I met Ava at work and we dated for about three years. I didn't know what was going on back then, but she got caught up in a project that was covering up some illegal stuff. She was murdered a week before I was going to propose... fell in front of a train in the station were we worked." Okay, maybe I should have made her sweat. Having only one question might have been better than drudging up all the memories to try and get her to understand.

"Turned out a couple cops were being paid off, and they tried coming after me next. The sick bastard gave me her autopsy fi..." It was getting harder to squeeze the words out. It wasn't just the memories now; it was the images. Flipping open that manila and seeing Ava's body torn into two. All that blood and the bits of her that I loved but never wanted to see. Seeing those words... "It said she was pregnant. I... I don't think she even knew."

I couldn't look at her and I'm not sure how long I've been staring at my ice cream. Her fingers were an odd sensation that was hard not to lean into as she brushed away the few tears escaping.

"I had no idea that was you," Cari said softly. "I heard about it years ago on the news. I... I'm so sorry, Jack." I tried not to numb it out again, but I couldn't let her see me like this. I didn't want to see me go back to this.

"It's just hard to talk about." I just have to push through it. "Family, friends, they all know and I've never had to tell anyone else. I never told anyone I started dating. It's just... I-"

Cari places a finger over my lips, quieting me. Not that I was exactly speaking in a normal level before. "Jack, I don't want you to feel like you have to push yourself to tell me. Okay?" She pulled her chair around to my side and sat. Linking our hands, she rested them in her lap.

63

"When and if you need to get it out, I will sit beside you, hold your hand like this, and listen. "

"I'm not trying to get you to stop opening up because it's too much or because I'm not interested in knowing you. I feel like I forced you to talk about her by making you come here. I could have left you go back to your hotel and rest, but I wanted to be selfish and I didn't really understand." Cari lifted our hands and gently kissed the back of mine. "I'm sorry, Jack."

We sat like that for a long time in silence. Her thumb gently ran across the back of my hand. Our ice cream started to melt and drip over the side of the bowl to the serving plate that caught it up. Shimmy Sam had started our way a couple times, but it must have been a look from Cari that kept him away. It felt like we had all the time in the world like this, and I couldn't be more thankful for having Cari.

"You're going to have two big bowls of soup," I said quietly. I just couldn't stay locked up in my head any longer without relapsing back to a hollowed-out shell.

"Soup?" I saw her confused look out of the corner of my eye and nodded towards our melting mounds. "Oh... I don't mind. It'll reduce my chances of getting brain freeze." Cari went silent for a while. "Are you okay?" It was a gentle question.

I nodded and reached back for the spoon. It wasn't lost on me that Cari still held my hand. There was no way I'd change that. If I ended up slopping because I was eating with my left hand, it wouldn't be the worst. I took a bite, feeling her eyes on me.

"Can we sort of... talk about something else?" I didn't know what else to say. My mind was lingering in one place and I knew it was putting Cari in an odd spot.

"Tell me about snow."

"Snow?" Okay, there's no way she just asked me about that. One, everyone knows about snow; and second, there was no way I was talking about the drug – which I knew nothing about – to a girl who looked like she never touched anything harder than a wine cooler.

She sighed. Score another one for failing, today. "You know, the white stuff. I lived in California my whole life and never really saw it. I mean, I saw it, but it snowed for maybe five minutes and then was gone an hour later. It's never really been that cold and you're from out east. It snows there, right?"

Cari had never seen snow. Real, honest to goodness, freeze your ass off, I-can't-see blizzard snow. If we hadn't just come from the most depression time in my life to this, I might have laughed. Instead, I poked the spoon back into the ice cream and got a dab. "It's really cold sometimes. Well, all the time for me. I can't take the cold without at least three layers of clothes and Ava... she used to tease me."

It still stung a little, but it wasn't as bad this time. It was like bungee jumping. You're fine falling, then the cord stretches and you think you're about to smash your head on the rocks; but then it pulls you back up, tossing you in an upward fall. It felt like I was digging myself out of that pit, and going back in to test the waters.

"Sometimes, it's dry and other times it's a little sticky from, like on a warmer day, were it melts a little on the way down. That kind of stuff is perfect for making a snowman." I feel her lean against my shoulder as she reaches out for her spoon. "It comes down so softly that it creates such a strange and wonderful world sometimes. It just coats everything," I smile a little, "and everything's so beautiful. It looks just like those winter holiday cards with the little cottage covered in snow and a smoking chimney."

"It sounds nice," Cari adds softly.

I nod. "It is. Except it has to be cold." Sighing, "I really, really hate the cold."

She giggled. It felt easy talking to her. It was just one hard question in the back of my mind. I knew that I could have a future with Cari when I figured out how we were going to make this work. I could see Cari's future with me, but I couldn't see her past. It had scared me as much as relieved me when I found out she was single. But how could a girl like that really be single without some huge baggage she was dragging behind her?

"So you know my story. Why've you been single?"

Cari took a scoop of ice cream. Shit. And a big scoop too! She must not want to tell me. So I watched and waited for Cari to finish, all the while working up bad scenario after bad scenario in my head. Was she hit? Did someone cheat on her? Could it have been a small penis that made her laugh and dump the guy? ... and what would she think of mine when – if – she saw it? It wasn't like I had a permanent hard-on and was hung like an elephant from some kind of book she might have read. That industry definitely made dating life rougher.

"No special reason." I felt her shrug. "It's not like the guys I dated were horrible. It's just that they weren't the right one for me. You know, nothing huge like the guy being a slob or being too clingy or they had skeletons in the closet or a closet gay or even a crazy ex. Well, there was one with a crazy ex, but she wasn't too bad," she reached for another scoop, "because she was just pregnant with his kid. That was about the most drama I've had.

"I've been lucky in that sense, but there's so many things that you just want to have someone with you for, you know?" Cari savored the sweet for a moment before continuing. "Like my best friend's wedding. Of course you're going and, no, you don't really need a date. But with all that love in the air, you want your own... and not some creepy old uncle with drifting hands on your ass while you play nice and dance with him. It's not like I've avoided dated. Well, except this night in the bar where some stranger from across the country tried charming me."

"So, what about me?" I smiled softly, hopeful. "Do I get a chance?" It sounded like I might have a shot. I was the exception that night. I got her to meet me the next day, and every day after that. I got her here, now, and so close to me.

Her eyes found mine and I tried to search them for an answer. Anything to brace myself for what was coming next. Cari was either going to save me or crush me. "Of course you do. I kind of just agreed to be your sexy kitty cat," she teased. It might have been a jab but, damn, if it didn't feel good.

"*My* sexy kitty cat." I must have had a shit-eating grin. Giving her hand a little squeeze, I added, "I like how that sounds." I love how that sounds. I hadn't expected to find a girlfriend out here. Hell, I never expected to find anyone half as good as her to be with. Maybe Ava and Train were right – San Francisco was saving me.

"How are those legs?" She looked at me. Was she biting her lip? It was hard to tell if that was adorable or sexy.

"I think they're good now, but I reserve the right to change my answer. Why do you ask?" This was going to be the part where she made me chase her to the bridge. We had gotten our rest but now we had to run off the million calories from what little ice cream we ate before it turned into a messy puddle.

"You'll see." She got up and instantly I felt cold from the space between us. How could I miss her already when she wasn't even a foot away? Cari held out her hand for mine and I was too blinded from her to question it. Taking her hand meant touching her, and I needed that right now. Even if it meant she was going to end up killing me, it wasn't a bad way to go...

Chapter Five

Cari smirked as she dangled my key card in front of me. She had swiped it out of my back pocket. Never had I thought she'd back me up against the elevator and blank my mind with a kiss. That was supposed to be my job. The worst part was that I hadn't even felt her go into my pants. When a girl reaches into my pants, I want to feel it.

"You little thief." I couldn't let her run off with anything else. Although it felt like she already claimed my heart long ago.

She laughed and backed against the door as I stalked closer. "And what ya going to do about it?" Oh, there was a lot I wanted to do to her... I mean, about it.

Snatching the key card, the door clicked open and I pushed her backwards into my room. Her hands ran down from my shoulders. Her fingers splayed across my chest, brushing against my nipples, causing my cock to twitch. Damn. I thought only girls got any enjoyment out of those. They were useless on me, but there was just something about Cari that made me want to ask her to do it again.

Her hands didn't falter as her legs hit the edge of the bed. "Jack, I want..." Cari hesitated. Ice cream? Oranges? A unicycle? Waiting the two seconds for her courage to build up was torture. "I want this, Jack. I want you."

There weren't sweeter words on the planet right now. "I want you too." I leaned in, finally, so my lips can brush against hers. "I've wanted you for so long, my sexy kitty cat."

Her laugh caught me off guard and caused her lips to brush so tantalizing against mine. "Call me that again, big daddy." Big what? As much as I hated to stop this, there was just no way.

"Please tell me you're kidding." I never understood why girls ever called their lovers "daddy" and I didn't want to start down that rabbit hole. Maybe it had to do partially with the fact that I almost was, had been, a dad. I'm sure Cari was just playing with what we started at the ice cream shop.

"Cari, that's a huge turn off. I –" A slender finger is all it took to silence me. I feel like I owe her an explanation. It's rotten timing. It was probably a mood killer too. It was just that I wanted this to happen and for her to know it wasn't really her.

Soft lips replaced the tease that ran over my lips and along my jaw. "I'm sorry." It was just a whisper. Something more felt than heard. It wasn't that I needed an apology, but I could tell that she hadn't meant it like I had thought. "Let me make it up to you."

Oh god.

Her hand slid down the front of my shorts and gave me a firm handshake. I never had a girl cop a feel and turn me on more. I never had a girl like Cari in my arms. Period. Groaning, I couldn't help but push into her touch. Hearing her soft laughter didn't affect how this felt. I was with Cari and that little noise was one part of her that I loved; and not something that could ruin what was going on between us.

Her name slipped out as a soft moan; rewarded with a slightly deviant smile. Her hand teased down the front of me as she sank down to the edge of the bed. Cari was a tease as her fingers drag up over my straining groan and hooked into both my shorts and boxer briefs to pull them down my legs. A small gasp fled her lips as I hung free. I knew it wasn't because I was hung like a horse or perma-hard. I was worried that I wasn't up to the standards in Cari's head, until I risked a glance down to see her face. Her eyes were glued to my arousal and a smile was on her face. Half gasp, half hiss. My eyes roll close as she wraps a hand around me.

"I'm going to love this." The sound of her voice sounded heavy with desire. My brain tried to wrap around her words as she wrapped her fingers up and down the length of me. I groaned as I felt something slick darted over the tip. "I'm going to make you so hard. I'm going to make you feel so good, Jack."

Her tongue ran along the underside of my cock and I shiver. I had been half-mast when Cari freed me, but she was changing that fast. Her thumb rubbed circles under my pliable cock, causing more of my skin to brush against hers – Cari's cheek was so soft. She turned her head slightly and the inside of her mouth was a newfound heaven.

"Oh god." I wanted to give in and come right now. Cari was too much and not enough at the same time. She rolled my balls in one hand as the other ran down my cock from her greedy mouth. "Cari," I groaned. It was almost painful to feel this good. After this morning, I shouldn't. I didn't deserve her, this.

She obviously felt the same. Cari hummed her agreement and it felt like nothing I've ever known. She barely had me down her throat again. I wasn't going to make it. There was no way that I was going to enjoy this without her. I needed her coming with me. I wanted her with me, even if it would kill me to have her stop this.

"Cari." I let my hand brush over her hair and thought for a moment that I could just grab her ponytail and pull her down on me. It was tempting, if I didn't want this girl for more than just tonight. My fingers graze her cheek before tilting her chin up to look at me. That almost was ended me. Her eyes were half-lidded with lust and her tongue kept sliding along me even though I had stopped her.

"I want hold you as we come apart." For a moment, she was completely still. Not a single breath; not even a blink. "You're my girl and this isn't a one-time thing. I don't want you on your knees. I want you in my bed, saying my na-" Cari was up and her lips were suddenly on mine and, for a second, I couldn't remember anything else but how soft and sweet her lips tasted. She didn't say a word as she moved to the bed.

Cari scooted up the mattress with little but a sexy smile on her body. To know that she really wanted me blew my mind. A beautiful girl, inside and out, was laying herself out for me. And I wasn't about to make her wait. My hands went to the hem of my tee and yanked it over my head. It landed somewhere on the floor with a muted thud, but my eyes were too focused on the girl in my bed to care where it went. All I could think about was getting closer to her again.

Her eyes watched my mediocre muscles flex as my body crawled up the bed slowly lowered to cover hers. Softly, I stole a kiss. To feel her hands run up my chest and around to my back couldn't compare to anything. It wasn't just what she was doing; it was having Cari's hands on me, like she couldn't get enough. She pulled me down and I could feel how much was still between us.

The hot shirt that started my dirty thoughts now turned me into a fumbling mess as I tried to get my hands under it. That damn clingy thing was making me out to be an inexperienced putz with Cari and that's definitely not how I wanted her to think of me. I want to be the one that drove her crazy and ruined her for every other guy. I wanted her to want this to be more than a vacation fling and a long distance relationship.

I manage to peel the shirt from her soft curves and over her head. Her rosy breasts laid out for my eyes to devour. They made my mouth water and I desperately longed to taste them. I captured one between my lips and heard her gasp before fingers ran through my hair and over my scalp. I expected her to pull me down harder on her, but the tug on my hair wasn't pleasurable at all. Cari kept up until she popped out of my mouth. As pathetic as it was, I whined and glanced down at the glistening pebbled thing.

"Jack, I want you... I want you inside me... Please, I can feel you..."

As if to make her point, Cari rolled her hips up along my cock. Damn, as if I wasn't painfully hard before, my resistance was shot now. It was just that I wasn't done with her yet. I barely got a taste of her and I needed more. I needed to have her on my tongue. I needed... to remember that this just wasn't a one night thing. If she needed me now, I'd gladly give myself to her. There was always tomorrow for me.

I had to pull away to find a condom in my suitcase, but when I turned back around Cari had a surprise for me. She hooked her thumbs in the waistband on her tight shorts and pushed them down. Sweet Jesus... I toss the foil packet on the bed next to her and kneel between her legs, hands covering hers. My eyes struggle to stay on hers, knowing what I saw.

"Cari." It was barely a whisper, but she gave in. She had stripped me bare and taken me; I just wanted the same.

My fingers tugged down the shorts over her bare mound. If I had known that she went commando, we never would have left the hotel this morning. The shorts went flying over my shoulder, disappearing somewhere neither of us cared to note. There was nothing worth noting other than my aching cock and her perfect pink pussy that was about to get some much needed attention.

My lips brushed against her skin and Cari whined as I planted a kiss on the inside of her thigh. There was no way I was rushing this, even if she begged.

"Jack!" I smirked against her skin as I inched up her leg. Cari moved up onto her elbows, pleading with me through those blue orbs. I knew what would tantalize her more. She groaned, falling to her back, as my hot breath whispered over her delicate folds. God, I was so close; yet, I had to stay far away.

Her legs laid over my shoulders and tried to pull me in. "Oh, kitty cat." My laughs rolled over her skin and pulled another strained groan from her. The more Cari's heels dug in, the more I was determined to drive her crazy. But there was one more thing I wanted to drive Cari to do. Her fingers weren't in my hair, trying to hold me against her as she rode my face. The thought was never a turn-on until I saw Cari laid out for me. Her breasts were two perfect soft mounds and, as my gaze traveled back down, I saw something too perfect to pass another second.

I laid a gentle kiss to the top of her mound. It was like her body tensed in anticipation of what was to come at the same time it relaxed in knowing attention was coming. As my lips slide along her soft skin, Cari shivered. Her fingers invaded my hairline as my tongue slide between her folds and brushed against a bud that I was going to know a lot better.

"Oh, Jack," Cari sighed. That was twice she said my name tonight.

My tongue circled back and caressed that bundle of nerves. Her legs quivered and I had to wrap my hands around her thighs so she didn't get the idea to squeeze my head until it blew. There was only one way I was blowing, and she'd be going first.

Her fingers dug in as I sank deeper. She was the sweetest thing I ever tasted. "God, Cari," I whispered against her just before she gripped my hair and pulled me against her. Usually the women I was with didn't get demanding until their orgasm was upon them, and they wanted more. Cari took and tried to move us past that. I wanted to taste her on my tongue, flooding my mouth with all she was.

Every circle of my tongue elicited a breathy moan from her. It was good, but there was nothing special about it. Cari deserved something special. I slipped a digit in and her whole body arched from the surprise pleasure. She whined my name and begged for more. I watched as my finger disappeared inside her for a moment. Fuck, that was going to be my cock soon. I was ready to jump her now, but I forced my gaze away and sealed my lips around her mound. I sucked her clit as a second digit joined the party. Cari was writhing on the bed as my fingers scissor inside her and twist with each thrust.

"Jack! God, Jack," her voice was barely there, "don't stop! ... god, don't stop." Her body clenched around my fingers. "Oh, yes.... yes! Oh, god..." Her nails scratched my scalp as Cari got hold of my hair to pull me hard on her. And then she let go.

It was like she melted. Her legs went limp and the sweetest taste came on my tongue. Her fingers slowly untwined with my hair. I could still feel the pull long after her arms dropped to the bed beside her. She was soaked after that display, yet I knew she was too tender for much more right now. Damn my needy cock! All I could do was gently lick her clean and wait for a sign that she was back on Earth. The sight of her glistening in front of me was driving me insane. It was a guilty little trophy, seeing her like that. I smirked as I climbed up her body and reached for the condom. My cock brushed against her wet pussy and we both shivered.

"Jack," she whispered.

I leaned down to kiss her softly before ripping open the foiled packet. "I know, Cari. I'm hurrying."

Her hands ran over my chest and kept roaming over my stomach and into my treasure trail. They wrapped around my hands and helped roll on the rubber. It was the hardest thing to do.

"Cari, you sure about me?" It wasn't something that I wanted to ask. I didn't want to give her a chance to run. It would be a lie to say this would be enough.

She leaned up and kissed me. Her hand wrapped around me pulled me to her entrance. "Jack, I'm sure. I want you," she whispered against my lips.

Her legs wrapped around my waist and pulled me closer. I sank in slowly. Our eyes rolled shut together and a soft moan escaped us both. God, she felt better than I could have imagined. Her whole body gripped me and I had to stop. My forehead landed on hers as I fought my restraint.

"Cari, you're killing me."

She groaned when I stopped and now her eyes were once again a mystery. "I'm sorry, babe." Cari closed her eyes and rocked her hips up against me. "You just feel... so good." She licked her lips...

... and I lost it.

The small amount of control that I had to stop evaporating. I sank in the rest of the way. Her legs tightened around me before dropping open after she adjusted. I gave her a moment – gave us a moment – to catch her breath. For doing so little, it felt like so much. Maybe it was just the girl beneath me or the final relief of being with her, but I felt ready to come. Slowly pulling out to slowly press in wasn't what I wanted. It was what I had to do to buy some time and take the edge off. And the way Cari was troubling her bottom lip between her teeth had to prove that she didn't mind either.

"Mhmm, Jack," it was becoming an addiction to hear her moan my name. "More." That one word. It wasn't entirely about what our bodies were doing. It felt like Cari had meant me. She really was mine. She wanted more of me.

I leaned down to kiss her as I changed our rhythm. I felt what she needed and I wanted to give her that Hollywood blitz. I knew that, with her, I'd be ready fast. It was just getting Cari to that edge to jump off with me. My lips brushed against hers a second time to soften the growing moans between us. Except Cari caught my bottom lip between her teeth and slowly let me release it.

"Damn..."

Cari hadn't ceased to surprise me. I hadn't expected that from her.

"I want more." A meek confession.

I stared down into her eyes as we moved. There was just something about the way she said it that sparked memories of her lips around my cock. She wanted more.

I grazed my thumb across her lip and watched as she sucked it. The feeling it stirred in my cock! This girl was something else, and watching my thumb glisten and vanish turned on something primal.

My hips jerked and rammed into her. Cari screamed out in surprise. I thought I might have accidentally hurt her until she moaned. Her fingers didn't run through my hair. Her nails didn't ran tracks down my back as she moved on the bed with me. They reached down and dug into my ass, forcing my hips harder and faster.

"Oh, god."

I wasn't in control anymore. I just needed to come, and her hands were pulling me deeper. She shivered beneath me and her body squeezed around me. It passed, but my only thought was to bury deep inside her. The grunts and growl that escaped my throat as I came seemed so foreign.

Our foreheads rested together a moment before I collapsed beside her on the bed. A gentle touch stopped my eyes from closing. I was so close to passing out. Her fingers brushed back the hair from my forehead after she snuggled into my side.

"That was great, Jack." She smiled softly. Those beautiful eyes drifted over my face before she kissed me softly.

"Did you come?" The moment of silence was enough. We didn't get that double whammy. "Cari," I start, but she cuts me off.

"It's fine, Jack. Sex was still great."

I huffed. Yea, right. Great. "I'm not going to leave you behind."

There was no way that I was going to take and then roll away. Cari was the only reason it was amazing. She tensed as my arm brushed against her breast while my digits sought her warmth. When two slipped inside, her breath caught. My thumb started with leisurely strolls around her clit. Whatever edge she lost felt like it was coming back, fast.

Her breathing wasn't so even. Her hips weren't so still as I matched the speed my cock had rammed into her. Each thrust had her moaning. Her eyes were rolling back, shut. My wrist popped from the pace. It didn't look like Cari wavered. But then her body relaxed a second before her legs suddenly clamped around my hand and went rigid through her orgasm.

"Jack!"

It was the loudest she ever called my name. And it was the only one that really mattered. I waited until her legs relaxed and she seemed to come back to earth before gently taking back my hand.

Her head lolled to the side as I moved to lay beside her. I doubted Cari could form words yet and I had to return the favor and beat her to the punch. "Watching you come is so damn hot, Cari. But next time you fall apart, I want it to be with me."

She rolled closer and snuggled back into my side. Cari kissed the place over my heart. Hell, I could feel it deeper than my skin. There was no doubt that I was in love with her. I knew that I couldn't tell her; not yet, anyways. Kissing her forehead, I wrapped my arms around Cari to keep her close.

"Jack." I glanced down at her. Was she going to say it first? "Do you have plans for next Friday?"

The answer didn't feel good to say. Especially after the blow to my ego of coming first. I didn't have plans, but I wasn't going to be available. I had to be back for the start of fall term. The best option for us still wasn't good enough for me. It meant being away for months and splitting the holidays between her and my parents. I'd have to start right away on the transfer papers and figure out living arrangements. It would be impossibly fast to move in with Cari, but I doubt we'd be separable.

All of it was more stipulation at this point. So I gave her the only firm answer I had. "My flight's in two days."

She rested her head on my chest. Over my heart, on her kiss. "Two days," she repeated quietly. Her hand rested near and drew small circles on my skin.

"I was thinking of maybe going to Sonoma County tomorrow. There was a brochure in the lobby for wine tasting tours. Is that something you'd be up for? My treat." I couldn't help grinning. My feelings had me filled to the brim and I wanted to tell her how much I loved her – at someplace romantic and not just after sex.

"Can't." Cari went quiet and still. "I have work."

That knocked me right down. "Well, maybe we can get together the next morning before I need to get to the airport then." I felt her shake her head. "Work," I sighed. Tonight could be the last time I saw her.

"Can someone swap shifts? Call off?"

"Jack." She sounded exasperated. Clearly that wasn't an option. I hated that it wasn't an option.

I sighed and just wrapped my arms around her. Why risk ruining what we have, and my chances of getting a little more of Cari in the morning before she had to leave for work? We could talk in the morning and come up with a plan. I kissed her forehead and let myself drift off.

Chapter Six

Mmm, Cari.

Last night... oh, last night. No words could describe it. It was everything and nothing at the same time, leaving me hungry for more – not just her body, every part of her. It was just so perfect. It was like we were made for each other. There wasn't even the bumbling that comes with a first with someone new. Somehow Cari knew me inside and out. And damn, if she hadn't ruined me. Every little noise, every little change on her face, the softness in her eyes when she looked up at me. It begged me to tell her those three huge words. I wasn't falling for Cari. I love her. I loved her and I never wanted to let her go.

Rolling over, I reach out to pull her close, to feel her soft skin flush against mine, to softly kiss her awake. My hand snaked over the bed and reached the edge. I must have rolled too far over or flipped myself around the bed. The last thing I remember was Cari on my left side. Mumbling, I reach over the other away. Spread across the bed, my hands touched edges and my stomach dropped. Opening my eyes, struck fear into me.

Where was Cari? Why was I finding nothing?

Bolting out of the bed, I didn't bother to wrap a sheet around my waist or cover up any. That was so low on my priority list and Cari knew what I looked like, felt like. She had to just be in the bathroom. That had to it. I was panicking for no reason. Things were fine – no, great – last night and I didn't have the chance yet to screw things up this morning.

The door was open. The light was off. Cari was gone.

She couldn't be gone. She wouldn't just up and leave me like this. I ran over to the night table and grabbed my cell. Thank god that I had her number. I tapped the smiling photo of my girl in prison and waited for her to pick up.

"Come on, Cari. Come on." My feet took me back and forth the length of the room. "Tell me you just got coffee. Tell me you're just..." It went to voicemail after three rings and my heart shattered. There was no way that it could do that unless... She didn't want to talk to me.

No.

This... this couldn't be happening. She...

I'm not sure that I ran out of that hotel fully dressed, much less matching. I knew that if I got to the street that I could see her, that I could catch up to her. I'd beg for her not to leave. Maybe I was horrible in bed, but I'd promise that I'd learn to be a better lover. I snored? Then I'd learn to stop breathing. I just couldn't let her walk away from me, from us.

I tried her phone again. Maybe it was just an accident. Maybe she meant to pick up but her finger slipped. Maybe... the call went straight to voicemail. No rings. No misunderstanding. Her phone was off and there was no way to turn around the fear she had shut off her phone to avoid me.

"Kitty cat, where are you? Baby, call me... plz." I sent the text. Her phone was off, but I couldn't give up. My hand quivered as I stared at the screen waiting for a reply, any reply. She'd send a text if she didn't want to hear my voice. She'd do that. She'd tell me that her battery died or the line at the bakery was super long or... she never wanted to see me again.

The worst part was not knowing what went wrong. I didn't do anything, but I knew it had to be my fault. What could I have done to make her bolt? My mind ran through everything that happened yesterday. Maybe she was just out for a run. She had the right clothes. Running upstairs, I changed quickly to a more normal outfit. I didn't want to risk missing her and letting this misunderstanding get more out of control.

I hailed a taxi and hauled ass to the Promenade. That was where she ran. She had to be here. I jogged from the street after paying the cabbie and headed down the path. I needed to see her. I couldn't wait for her to turn and make her way back to the trailhead. I jogged for almost a mile before slowing to take up residence on a bench.

Every runner that passed was another stab to the heart. My kitty cat wasn't any of them. None of them came close to having her stunning ocean eyes or golden hair or heart-stopping smile. Not even in the dying light. I checked my phone, desperate to see any notification that she was out there and looking for me. Not a glimmer of life. Just a measure of time lost.

A day without Cari.

The dim morning light reflected off the screen of my phone. I don't know why I was still trying when it didn't matter. Cari hadn't texted, called, or came back. I had holed up in the hotel to wait for her, not wanting to risk truly losing her. She had left, and she left me with nothing. Nothing but the three words staring back at me from my last text.

"I love you."

I told her. She knew it, felt it, and now heard it from me. I had begged, apologized, and professed how I felt. And Cari shut me out. I ran a finger over her smiling face and wished I could touch her one more time. Pull her into my arms and know she was still going to be mine. To kiss her and know that she felt the same and that my heart wasn't just destroyed.

My flight left in six hours. I had pictured today entirely different. Cari would either have spent the night again or have met me downstairs. We'd grab coffee at the bakery down the street and nibble pastries as we took one last walk around town together. She'd be glowing and wearing a bright smile as she sipped her coffee and chatted over the rising steam in the cool morning air. We'd grab an early lunch and talk about us. Would we Skype or call every night? Email and text? Would she visit the East Coast and when would I be able to come back out to see her?

Crappy hotel room coffee sat ice cold on the night stand and all I had was a one-way conversation on my cell phone. My last hours on this half of the country that were supposed to be filled with Cari were as empty as I felt. She wasn't talking to me, but somehow I had to see her. I had to understand what went wrong and figure out how to get my girl back. If I just knew where she was...

7:24 AM.

I checked my phone again. Had two days already passed since my attempted murder? Cari had said she ran every day, and that beautiful body was proof of it. I knew where she liked to run. That was where we were going before my legs turned to jelly and my lungs ran off. Maybe, if I could just get there, I could wait and see her on her run. I'd get the chance to talk to her. There was still hope. I just had to get to the trailhead before she did.

It felt like everything was against that though. The one day I needed to be early, everyone was taking their time. The front desk had called for a taxi while I checked out but, with the morning traffic, I still lost ten minutes. I swear every light turned red and the Boy Scouts were staging a badge earning event for the elderly. Grandma after grandpa were in the crossing walk when we needed to turn. It was getting so close to eight o'clock. While it was early and the start of the work day, it would almost be too late for runners.

The cab driver was disgruntled enough by my constant begging for a faster route or to just run over an elderly person – just a little – to get me there faster. It was probably why the fare had cost me so much, but that wasn't important. I needed to talk to Cari. At this point, I'd almost be okay with just seeing her from afar. From my perch on one of the benches lining the trail, I waited, suitcase in tow. There were blonde runner after blonde runner, to the bridge and back. None of them seeming to pay me any mind or pause in their daily ritual. None of them Cari. By eleven, the crowd had thinned to almost non-existent.

I just didn't understand. She said that she ran every day. This trail was her favorite. Even if I was too late to catch her on the way out, I should have at least seen her running back towards town. It was like she didn't exist, never existed. She was like the Tooth Fairy. A pretty little thing that I believed in. She made my dreams come true; and then, I find out that she was just a figment of the imagination. A beautiful lie that I fell in love with.

And time had run out. If I didn't leave right now, there was no way that I'd be able to catch my flight. It was laughable to think that forty-eight hours ago I hadn't care. I would have missed the flight, and the one after it, just to spend a couple more hours with her. Now, heartbroken, I couldn't get away fast enough.

It was easy to find a taxi off of Fisherman's Wharf. It wasn't easy to recall how I managed to get from there to the front door of my apartment. I had my suitcase in one hand and the keys in the other. Inside, it was like nothing had changed. No wonderful woman shaking up my life and leaving me in shambles. Minus the suitcase that I ditched by the door, it didn't look like I was gone a day. There was still no food in the fridge and a pile of laundry waiting in the corner.

Chapter Seven

I wasn't sure about any of my actions or reasoning. Why I chosen to go back to school was a bit beyond me. The investigation against Officer Dunn and the senator was over with for the most part. My life – or what of it was left – was set. I'd never have to work another day in my life. I could just stay in my apartment and not deal with anything. Well, except my mom coming over to check up on me and try to set me up on more blind dates. And after Cari, holing myself up in my own little prison had been so much more enticing.

Sighing, I grab the messenger bag and pull it over my shoulder. It's an oddly heavy load for a photography major. I thought all I would need would be a camera and just maybe a book or two to tell me how to set up shots. Instead I have about five, including one just on the history of photography. That must be the driest book to read, and I had only flipped through the first ten pages. It was going to be a long semester.

I decided that I would live in the dormitory. I wasn't sure why I wanted to live back in the dorms when my first time around as an engineering undergraduate hadn't been that great. I was never engaged in any of the special events for residents, or maybe I was just too self-absorbed in my world to go out. It was just my luck that I'd want to be around people again and then not to have been assigned a roommate. Well, I guess – according to campus housing – I was but they dropped out at the last moment.

It meant that I had no one waking me at some ungodly hour with their alarm to make an early morning class. But it also meant that I didn't have anyone reminding me to get my ass to class. Case and point. I was now running late on my first day. I was rushing when I turned a corner and ran into a body that when tumbling down to the floor with me.

"What the fuck?" A groan came from my left.

I look over to see a bob of brown hair shake in an attempt to get all that hair out of her face. Shit. I ran into a girl. If that didn't make me feel like a dick, then I didn't know what would anymore.

"Listen, I'm really sorry." I get up and extend my hand out to help her up. I thought I was being gentlemanly, but she completely ignores it and gets up to brush herself off.

"How about you just watch where you're going, asshole?" She leans down to pick up her couple of books that had gone flying in the tumble. "I could report you to campus security for sexual harassment."

Oh shit. I couldn't tell if she was serious or not. But the fact was that she could be. She was a woman and no matter what, I was a guy and guilty by default. I needed to come up with something fast to make it up to this woman. I didn't want the rest of my college career to be marred and miserable because of a misunderstanding.

"I'm sorry. I was just running late to class." Maybe I should just skip and try again tomorrow. "I've learned my lesson and will never run into someone again." Crap. That was just a line of bull to pacify her when it was going to be impossible to ever prove. That wasn't making things right. I was screwing this up more and she was going to report my stupid ass.

I held out my hand again. "My name's Jack Havest. I'm sorry for running into you. If you let me, I'd like to try to make this up to you." Now how would I do that without making her think that this was my horrible attempt to pick her up – even though she was pretty. "How about Astro's Pizza and a chance to let bygones be bygones?"

She eyes me like I had six heads. Shaking her head slightly, those brown eyes roll. There was no way I was getting out of this now. This was just a failed attempt to ask her out or make her shrug it off and walk away rather than deal with me.

"Hannah Maloney." She didn't shake my hand, but she did give me the once-over. "I can do Saturday. Six o'clock. Bernal's Pizza instead." She starts to walk away, and I struggle to follow what is going on. "We'll meet here. Doubt you'd forget this corner, Jack Havest."

She disappears out the side door of the dorm. I wasn't so sure that I should be looking forward to making it up to this girl Hannah. She seems like a bitch but, then again, I did plow right into her. I could have just made her late to her class as well. Maybe I should take it like that and try not to go into Saturday with preconceived notions.

We were meeting up to grab pizza and, at best, be friends. Although, who was I kidding? Hannah was just going to use it as a free meal and then I'd never see her again.

Saturday night, I am alone at the corner. I haven't seen or heard from Hannah all week, nor had campus security been after me over the incident. I wasn't sure why I was standing here still at... 6:14 PM, but I was. Guess it was just to keep my word, even though no one was around to care or prove that I did. Guess this meant that I was off the hook. Although, when I started to walk away, the side door opened up and there she was. Black jeans and a school hoodie. This definitely was an obligation and not a date. I got her message clear. I felt slightly stupid in my khakis and black tee. It wasn't fancy, but it was one step up from her casual.

"Hey." She offers a timid smile. Guess she didn't think I'd still be here either.

I could point out that she was late, like I was that day, and that all bets were off. I already had a strange feeling about this. But I was a man of my honor, and I say, "Hey."

It is dead silence as I drive us down to Bernal's Pizza. With a bowling alley next door, I thought that we could have a little fun if she actually wanted to be friends and wasn't really a bitch. Now that whole idea seemed stupid. She wanted pizza and to be done. After all, how hard was it to say a word? Even if it was just small talk about the weather, it would have broken the awkward silence.

Chapter Eight

Hannah snuggled into my side. Football. Who'd ever think that I'd be watching a football game? But I had to at least try. There was so many things that I've tried for girls and hoped it would help our relationship last. Ava got me in the snow and addicted to a drink called Jack Rose. The girls from my wanderings helped me get the courage to try their local cuisine, not all of which should be legally allowed for consumption. Girls in my class just wanted to bend me like a pretzel as their model, so I got into yoga. Cari had been one in a long line, and she had managed to make me almost kill myself by going on a run. In retrospect, sitting comfortably on my couch to watch big, sweaty guys fight over a ball with a girl and a beer didn't seem like any effort at all.

"So who's playing?" I couldn't tell with the team colors. I could only guess the Eagles because Hannah was a huge fan. "I know the Eagles are, but who's in the white?"

She laughs and I know a lecture's coming. "Jack, it's silver."

She moves to try and get comfortable... again. Honestly, how could she not be comfortable on this couch? This couch rocks. It was just soft enough and had the right amount of firmness. Plus the suede fabric just made it feel warm and homey. The only thing she could possibly find uncomfortable was me, and that couldn't be it.

"I just got done telling you. We're playing the Dallas Cowboys. They're 4-3 so far this season with a semi-decent starting line-up all because the Eagles fucked up during the draft and passed on McKillian."

She's rolling her eyes. I don't even need to look at her to know that. Hannah managed to answer one question, but created a half dozen more. Like who was McKillian? I could ask, but the pre-game show already started and it's sacrilegious to talk during the game. I don't know why, but Hannah's trying my patience. She should be happy that I'm finally giving into her nagging to watch a stupid game and drop whatever attitude reared its head just now. I just nurse my beer and hope it'll be over soon.

But three hours later, and countless curses and screams later, I'm still stuck on this couch watching titans run into each other over a tiny ball. I gave up long ago trying to learn and enjoy the game. Hannah was beyond her limit of being helpful anyways; unless it was screaming critiques at the referees hundreds of miles away. I was just hoping for someone to start a fight, or at least get a concussion... something. How anyone could be such a fan over a game so stupid was beyond me.

I shouldn't have been surprised when Hannah, finally, called it a night. The Eagles were down by seventeen with five minutes left in the game. There was no miracle that could save them now, especially now that Dallas had possession with no downs. She got up and headed to my bedroom. I could tell that she was raiding my closet for something to sleep in; and, for some reason, the idea just further irritated me tonight. Hannah was pretty cool with my baggage and my quirks. I know I shouldn't complain when she was a pretty fantastic girl, and hot. It was just that it hadn't felt right for a while now, and I wasn't sure how to either fix us or break us. Maybe it was already too late.

"You staying?" I call, turning off the television and heading to my room.

"Yea. I don't have class 'til ten tomorrow. I'll have plenty of time to run home to change."

I walk in on her pulling my shirt over her head. Seeing her bare back, I'm not even tempted to touch her. I don't understand it. The last girl I slept with just needed a tight pair of pants and I was ready to jump her. No, it wasn't even something as provocative as that. What did Hannah lose that Cari's memory could still beat out? I shouldn't get more turned on with my past than my girlfriend standing in front of me with nothing but her panties and my t-shirt. Nothing about how I feel right now makes me want to crawl in that bed with her, even if I know nothing going to be going on... tonight.

Hannah beats me into bed and has that look on her face. She's not excited over the fact that I not only have pajama pants on but a t-shirt as well. There's no skin for her to make contact and spark something. I hadn't truly realized it until she mention it before her hand slipped under the shirt to run over my stomach.

"What's wrong with you tonight?" She's staring at me. "First, you act like you hated the game when I know there's no way you could have. And now you're bundled up like a blizzard's coming. What is it?"

A groan escapes before it can be quelled. "Nothing's wrong," I attempt first. Maybe she'll accept that and drop it, but she keeps her gaze on me.

"Is it your ex? Did she make you watch a game and now she's on your mind?" It would make sense. That was unless she had actually listened to what I've said about never seeing a football game. But the fact that she jumps to Ava isn't making me want to open up to her. I know that I haven't told her much about what happened, but I never wanted to with her and it's a button that she loves to push.

"Ava wasn't my ex. She was my fiancé." Maybe defending her like that and goading where our relationship had been going is a bad idea with Hannah. I should know that her past relationships weren't perfect and try to be gentler with how I'm handling things now. Her last boyfriend had cheated and kept lies, but if she was comparing the two of us then there was no way we were going to even last the semester. "And no, she wasn't on my mind until you brought her up. It's been going on four years and I told you that I'm passed all that. I hated the game because football is a stupid, boring game. The only thing worse is NASCAR. I take that back. At least in NASCAR I can hope for a crash or fire or cars flipping. I just spent my night watching sweaty fat guys run into each other."

I know that I'm going to say something that I regret, but I'm sure every word out of my mouth tonight is already in Hannah's bag to quote me later. "I... I just don't feel like being here with you tonight. I just... Hannah, I don't know what we're doing together. It hasn't felt right lately." I sigh, feeling the bed shift. Before I know it, her arms are around me.

"I can go, Jack. I just thought you'd want me around tonight. It was just that she died today and I thought you'd need me." I can hear the hurt in her voice. When she puts it that way, I feel horrible. Hannah's just trying to be thoughtful. That was just who she was. So she got a little carried away with the game. So she just assumed what state I was in. To be honest, maybe if I had realized it was Ava's death anniversary, I might have needed her. I'm too exhausted to feel anything more than the guilt for my thoughts. Hannah was just being the perfect girlfriend and she didn't deserve how I was being tonight.

"I'm sorry, Hannah. I just..." Just what? Feel guilty? Lost? Her logic made perfect sense to everything but how seeing her nude back made me feel. I felt nothing knowing she was ready to be enjoyed.

She kisses me cheek, and all's forgiven. For now. "Why don't you tell me about her? Tell me how she died at least."

Talking things out always worked for nightmares and things weighting on the mind. But Ava was special. Talking about her never helped anything. It almost made it all that much worse each time my mind went back there. "Not tonight, Hannah."

She lets it go – again – as I lay back in bed. She has to be wondering if there's anything else that I'm keeping from her, or maybe she's starting to think I murdered Ava. She just lays back and curls up with me, trying to fix us and turn tonight into any other. While Hannah can fall asleep easily, I'm stuck thinking about the women in my life – Ava... and Cari.

Chapter Nine

Hannah sits down next to be on the couch and hands me a bowl. Tonight, she decided it was time that I taste one of her favorite family recipes. It looks delicious and the pasta is perfectly al dente.

"Avery Mayfield is supposed to be speaking tonight," she says casually.

I have no idea who that is, but apparently it's someone important in Hannah's world. I'm guessing that she wants to watch that instead of a show I'd be interested in. It wouldn't be the first time we sat around listening to some politician talk. That seemed to be one of the hazards of dating a law student.

Hannah flips through channels until an African American woman is shown speaking.

Avery Mayfield, 37. Maryland.

Or so the ticker across the bottom of the screen said. She was just being introduced when we got to the news channel. Beside me, I could feel Hannah snuggle against me and start to dig into her bowl of bowtie pasta.

"There's a time when we need to ask ourselves – How much is enough? "An eye for an eye" was logical in biblical times and in Shakespearean lore. It's what turns family, neighbors, nations upon themselves."

I had to admit – this woman had a way with words. Hannah was totally transfixed next to me.

"Our nation was once under British rule. Conditions were just as unfair. Attack could come without warning, then and as we see each night on the news. We fought for freedom. We fought for equality... and we got that. We became a nation, a band of brothers. The color of our skin or the beliefs we held did not separate us then. So why so we hold the past hatred so fresh and high in our thoughts? Our nation has peace with England and moves forward each day. For those that once fought against us, suppressed us, we've let transgressions lie in the past. Why can't we grant our brother the same?

"Like Martin Luther King Jr, I have a dream. I have a dream that one day we can move pass our past. That one day we can interact indifferently and without fear of being attacked based on our differences. One day, we shall lay down the hatred and retribution of the past generations that has long been unaffected on our lives.

"I was not touched by discrimination, slavery, stripping of basic human rights. Nor has my parents... and their parents' parents. As a nation, we can never forget, and mustn't. We need to let go of unjust hatred. We need to forgive our brothers for what was done and what is being done. Starting today, we all need to look at our lives and

see whom owes us for personal wrongdoings. And, when we go to take that retribution, we stop and forgive. We end the cycle of violence and hatred.

"This march is not a protest on Washington. This march is a demonstration of us. This is the first time when the people need a change. A change by the people, for the people. We walk for our future. We walk for ourselves."

Chapter Ten

"Friday there will be an exam on the composition and nuances of photographical effects. All the natural phenomena will be covered and expect to expand on the usages of color cast, motion blur and be able to deconstruct a photograph for all processes performed. "

I scribble down a reminder in my planner. I had no clue what *"Photographical Deconstruction and Application"* was from the long list of courses the advisor gave me months ago, but it's quickly become my favorite. There's just something exciting about digging around an image and learning the pixels and settings that make a great photograph. Maybe it has something to do with my life with Ava, before I tried to really bury the past.

Heading out of class, I spotted Hannah waiting for me. "Hey, honey."

She doesn't have a huge smile for me. Obviously our spat a couple nights ago hasn't been forgotten. I can't help but wonder if this isn't her way of checking up on me. Was she really expecting to walk in on me screwing some sorority sister in the shower like her ex?

"I thought you might want to grab lunch. My class got cancelled and I figured that I'd see you before I go." Go? Was she breaking up with me? The idea wasn't devastating, oddly. My blank stare must be obvious that I have no idea what she's talking about. There was nothing down in my planner, so it couldn't be something too important. "I'm going with Gina to DC for the hearing?"

My brain tries to rapidly recall anything she's told me about this. "Congressionally hearing?" I hope that I guessed right. With Hannah being a Political Science major, it was picking a needle in a haystack when guessing about anything related to the Capital.

It must have been right enough. "They're going to address the primary education funding and are proposing reformations that are going to reduce the rate of middle class performing at academic standards. I can't believe how stupid those radicals are being, just because they want to bring a standardization to home schooling... They're going to reduce every public school student to a sub-par education and destroy their collegiate opportunities," she exasperates.

Her passion was one thing that drew me to Hannah. She always had something to fight for and seeing her love for something had made me realize that there had to be something worth it out there for me. I had thought if I could have that spark for her, then I'd have that fight for everything else. I had the spark in me. Or at least I thought I did... until San Francisco.

"So are you guys going to protest if they go through with it?" Her hand slips into mine as we head to the quad where the food trucks usually line up on the curb. She nods and I can't help but question her decision. "You know that you could end up in jail. You could make it on some list and be banned from airports."

Hannah shrugs. "It would be worth it though."

"We won't be able to see each other." Again she shrugs and I wonder what we're doing together. Is this still about the fight or has the fight for each other ended? It feels like we're at an impasse. Maybe being apart this weekend might be a good thing. Maybe it's what we need to get back on track. Glancing over at Hannah, I know that I still like her, but I'm not sure it's deeper than admiration anymore. She's beautiful and happy and she's made me want to change to become a better person.

She gives me a quick peck on the cheek before running off to her favorite food cart while I wait in line at a Chinese food one that's grown on me. It feels like that's all anything does – grows on me. Maybe I should start listening to that nagging voice. Maybe this fight isn't about us, but where we're going.

I glance over at her, seeing her up on her tiptoes to order through the truck's window. Hannah's what I would have wanted for myself. She's someone that I've managed to semi-live with. Why isn't it working out how I would have wanted it? I didn't want to have to wonder if our relationship, the one I wanted and thought we had, was all just in my head. I didn't want to have to wonder because I was pretty sure that I knew the answer already.

The truck vendor called my name as the order came up and shook my thoughts away. Maybe we could make things work out once Hannah got back. Maybe things could change...

Her bag is so damn heavy, but I'm forced to haul it into my apartment. I have to take my punishment quietly so I don't piss of Hannah again. She finally got over my comment about being right. That's why it's Monday night and she's finally getting home after waiting the weekend in a holding cell for a judge to dish out bail and a fine.

"Got any pizza left?" Hannah walks over and yanks open the refrigerator door. I had mentioned on the phone that I had ordered us Bernal's Pizza – the best pizza in town as far as I was concerned. It was her favorite that she got me hooked on. Of course that was Saturday, when I was making plans to wow her and give things another try.

"Cassidy and Mark saw it when they stopped by to tell me you weren't coming on the eight o'clock train. They stole the few pieces that were left." At least her friends had bothered to tell me before I sat at the train station for hours waiting for her.

Sighing, she grabs the bologna and starts to make a sandwich. "Those assholes! I can't believe they stole my pizza." Hannah slaps the slice of bread on top to finish the sandwich before ripping out a bite. "I can't believe that you let them take my pizza."

Wow. This wasn't my Hannah. I had to try and convince myself of that. She had to be just tired or... something. This girl wasn't the one I'd spend months dating. The last couple months couldn't have been a waste of time, and I needed to prove that to myself. I wrap my arms around her waist as I kiss her neck. "I've missed you, you know."

Hannah laughs and leans back against me. "Oh yea?"

She takes another bite of her sandwich before turning in my arms to kiss me. I can taste the saltiness of the bologna on her mouth as she pushes her tongue past my lips and brushes it along my own. It's not the type of missing I had meant, but I do nothing to stop it. Ending it now would end us, and I promised myself that I'd try.

Her hands weave through my hair as she pushes her body against mine. Not just pushes to get against me. Pushes to direct me. I feel something press back against my legs and my hand leaves her side to feel for what I've been trapped against. The table. My heart sinks as I realize that she's desperate to make up for missing me, but I don't want this at all. Making out, I could handle. But her intentions are so clear.

"Table, now," she whispers in my ears as she grants me a brief respite to fill my lungs again. Hannah moves out of sight and I hear papers, and probably my cell phone, cascade to the floor. The table rocks a little against my thigh as she climbs on.

I can't do this.

Her hand reaches for mine and a shred of me hopes that she just wants to up the ante on our make-out session. But she pulls me between her legs and her hands start fumbling with my belt. She's managed to get it off before I can even come up with words to say and, then, her lips are on mine.

"Jack, I need this," she whispered.

Her need was evident. When her hand disappeared inside my jeans and wrapped around me, I forgot why I wasn't jumping at this. It's been weeks since the last time, between our class schedules and her time in jail. I needed this too. We just needed to reconnect.

The pants drop and then her tee, but not before a condom from my wallet got tossed next to her on the table. Her hands worked to get my shirt off as her bra went flying off. A soft moan escaped her as my hand brushed over her pebbling nipple. She leaned up to the touch, pressing her breast against my palm.

I used to marvel at how my touch could paint her creamy tone in soft pink hues until I pushed me over that explosive cliff. Seeing her eager on my table like a laid-out meal for me to devour, it didn't get my blood pumping fast enough. I wasn't sure if I could get it up this time but it looked like I'd have just enough flowing to roll the rubber over me.

"I missed your fucking cock so much." Oh, no... She was starting with the dirty talk. I could feel my erection turning limp. I didn't want it, not tonight. "I've been a bad girl. Fucking teach me a lesson."

I bruised my lips as I crushed them against hers. The talk had to end if there was any hope of following through with this. We had to get through this to save our relationship.

While my mouth tried to distract her forceful tongue, I rolled the protection over my uninterested appendage. Years. Years I had waited for sex to happen and now someone was begging me. I had to give up on me and let a horny teenage version take the wheel. I edged inside her, hearing a quick gasp as I gave in and took her early. Hannah wasn't as wet as I'd liked, but she needed this. We needed this. She moaned as I dove back into her again.

"Yeah, fucking take me hard like that!"

Her hand reached to squeeze my ass. I bowed to her desires. I raced on, letting her think it was her doing that egged me on. I just needed a release. I wanted this to end so badly.

"Oh, Jack. Yes! Fucking take me, you beast!"

I could feel the back of her hand brush against me as she sped herself closer to that cliff. Her hand was rapid on her clit between us. Did Hannah pick up how I felt or was she hungry only for her own end?

"Oh, god! That's it! Harder! Harder!"

She was pushing up to meet each thrust while pulling me deeper with her heels on my ass. If I hadn't blocked her out, I wouldn't be feeling this close. Hannah loses it, screaming out my name as her body pulses around me and pushes me over the edge. A low groan is all that gets out of me. It is all that I would allow with how against this. I'm feeling.

Hannah just isn't *it* for me anymore.

I can't believe that's the thought I have when I pull out of her. It should be how great she is or how fun she is to be around. Hell, even thinking how sexy that body is or how crazy sex with her is. Instead, I'm going to be a bastard in her eyes.

"Thanks, Jack. That was just what I needed." She kisses my cheek before hopping off the table to get cleaned up. I listen as she hums on her way to my bathroom.

Her words left me with another bad taste. Those words just twisted my gut with the thought that she was using me. As ridiculous as that sounded, realizing there was no connection gives it traction. Hannah never got into pet names; and hell, how hard was it to throw out a 'babe' or a 'hun' every now and then? I had questioned our relationship for a while and I should have realized it sooner that we weren't working. I had let it go on too long.

"I'm going to grab a shower." The water turns on. It's not Hannah asked me to join her that has me heading over.

She's starting to get into the shower when she sees me at the door. A smile starts on her face when she thinks that this is heading only one way. "Hannah, you need to grab everything."

Halfway in, she steps out. "What do you mean? Grab everything for a shower? I was just going to steal a little of your body wash."

But that wasn't what I was getting at. There was no good way to say it, but I can't not clear things up. If I just blow it off, this relationship would just keep going on in a pointless circle. Hannah might be alright with this, but I deserved better. Hell, I deserved to be head over fucking heels in love with someone like...

I hadn't thought about Cari in months. Now she was someone that I should be with. She was someone that got what a relationship should be about. She was the girl that

I should have spent the last several months trying to convince that I was The One.

"I can't do this anymore, Hannah."

"Do what exactly, Jack?" Her arms cross over her chest, and she knows. She knows exactly what I can't do anymore. Hannah's just hoping I'm not going to be that bastard that pumps and dumps. I'm going to destroy the man she knows me to be.

My hands just hang at my side. I wouldn't blame her if she hit me. I kind of expect it. Taking a deep breath, the words come out. "Hannah, I don't want to see you anymore. We're not working and we're not happy with each other. We've both changed so much since we met and-"

The slap reverberated off the tile of the bathroom. "You fucking bastard!" Hannah shoved me again and again until the wall pressed against my back. "You fuck me and then decide to toss me out? Suddenly, out of the blue, I'm not good enough for you!? You tell me you love me and then I get home and..."

Shit. That look says it all. It's so far from the truth, but it's already been confirmed in her mind. I'm cheating on her.

"Who is she?" It comes out sharper than I imagined Hannah could ever speak to me. "Tell me who the hell you're fucking? I'm going to shank that bitch."

Hannah's scrounging around for her clothes, and I'm glad for the reprieve from her focus. But that just means now she's posed to pillage my apartment. While she's abandoned me in the bathroom for a moment, I know I'm not safe there and I know it won't be long before she's back on the attack.

I could let her think that there's another woman. There'd really be no saving this doomed relationship then. Hannah wouldn't want to try to work it out or at least talk about it coming 'round. Letting her believe that I was cheating would destroy my reputation. There was no doubt that she'd tell her girl friends and they'd get it going around campus. I'd never be able to date again, and that was one of the perks of returning to school. But it was a perk that I no longer cared about. I didn't need a sea of chances to know what made me happy.

"How long?" The question cut through me. "Damn it, Jack! How fucking long have you been screwing around behind my back?"

"A month." The lie came out effortlessly. It had been at least a month since I felt the way about Hannah like I used to. It had been at least a month since I wanted this change. But if I really thought about it, it would have stretched back longer than that. The whole relationship was a cheating lie when I knew I still had feelings for that dime back on the West Coast.

Another slap stung my face, but it was nothing compared to how her tears tore at me. I had hurt Hannah deeply. I had turned into a repeat of the horrible ex-boyfriends that cheated on her. I had become her greatest fear, the only one she had.

Her lip may be quivering but her eyes were full and set with her anger. I had to shut my eyes. I had to afford me that tiny amount of protection because I was losing it.

I was so close to telling her there was no other woman; that basically, she was the other woman in my head.

"I hope that whore realizes what a fucking bastard you are and dumps your ass. You're going to fucking end up alone!"

The door to the apartment slams. I realize that I've been holding my breath and half my face is throbbing from her attacks. I can't help but be happy. I don't have to pretend and force things with Hannah. I can find someone easy to be with and who can always make me smile. I just have to figure out how to get on the next flight to San Francisco.

Chapter Eleven

Trying to get through security with a puffy, bruised face had not been the best idea in the world. Not only had TSA strongly requested to do the security screening in private, but local police got called to send over an officer. Apparently looking like I had with a beaten face and dressed as if I was fleeing something, which I had, set off many red flags. I either assaulted or killed someone, or had the same trouble coming my way. Assuring the officer that neither of those were the case and blaming the bruises on a slip in the shower, I was finally taking my first step back to the West Coast. Well, stumbling. Having tripped over a bin for the security scanner on way out, which had been barely peeking out from under the bench to sit and pull on shoes again. It only proved I was clumsy. But an escort to the gate was a little much. Then again, I would have missed the flight if they hadn't held it due to the "extenuating circumstances", and the golf cart ride definitely kept my wandering mind from causing more bodily harm. It was just hard to think of anything besides Cari. She managed to completely consume me with just the idea of seeing her again. And I needed to see her again.

I miss her golden hair and warm smile. There was a special way about her that I couldn't begin to describe. And then there was that one night we had together. It made waking up without her hell, but being with Cari was unforgettable. It had made the last days in San Francisco unbearable, but it was going to be so worth finding her and seeing that smile again. Of course there was a risk that Cari wouldn't be happy to see me. It was just that I couldn't remember a single time she hadn't beamed a smile my way.

It was that smile that got me through the eight hours of air time. It brought back memories of being a clumsy fool when I walked to the BART station at the airport. Only this time, I grabbed my ticket and boarded the train like I had been doing it my whole life. Just like last time, I checked into the same hotel. Cari had to be close. She was never late and I knew there were at least two Starbucks within walking distance from here. One of those places must be where Cari works. There was no doubt in my mind that I'd find her in time to take her out to dinner tonight – to make up and make it official. I knew Cari was meant for me. I just had to remind her of the week we were together. I just couldn't go to her like this.

The flight left me feeling dingy and less than my best. I couldn't have what possibly may be my only shot at getting Cari back while looking like I slept in my clothes for a week, and not smelling much different. A hot shower was able to remedy that and buy me a little more time to work out what I was going to say.

Stepping out of the hot stream, I grabbed a towel to wrap around my waist and wipe off the fog from the mirror. No bags under the eyes. Nothing in the teeth either. Hair was a little on the shaggy side. Running a hand back through my hair tamed it and gave me that sexy, effortless look. Well, at least that's what I was seeing.

"There's no way you're going to be able to say no, Cari." That handsome devil was smiling back at me in the mirror. I wasn't just another random stranger; we had a connection. "You're going to sit across a dimly lit table from me. We're going to talk like I never left. I'll walk you home and kiss you goodnight, hoping you'd ask me to stay." It would be great if Cari asked me in. After everything she told me about herself, I can only imagine how everything was going to look together. And maybe, I could even get to see that burlesque show... without any thongs.

I was going to have to pull on something worthy of tonight, and I hoped that I had managed to think of that in my rush to pack. There wasn't anything that had the wow factor I wanted but there was enough to put together a decent date outfit. Any good outfit starts at the base and, with what I hoped would be a night ending with Cari, I had to pull out the black boxer briefs first. Hannah had enough sappy romance books that I knew what was sexy. She quoted enough of it, hoping I'd change. I just didn't want to change for her. Oddly enough, it would match my black and white plaid shirt.

Khaki pants and a sharp orchid-colored sweater just fell into place. I hadn't felt nor looked this good in years, and it felt like I had truly gotten myself back.

There were a million things that I could do when I walked into Starbucks. There were so many good scenarios in my head that I couldn't even humor the negative. There was a Starbucks just a block away, and I was convinced that was the one. One of the street vendors called out and I couldn't believe that I hadn't thought of that before now. I stopped to see what he had in the large, white buckets.

I walk into Starbucks with a dozen golden-peach tulips bundled together with a deep purple ribbon. For having no other plan than walking in and having her run into my arms, I was actually pulling this off super well. The flowers matched well with my sweater; briefs matching my shirt. Heads turned to face me, but none of them was my California dime. There were two girls behind the counter that seemed glued to the flowers. I really hope that I haven't messed up by coming in like this and now was going to be fighting off everyone. There was only one thing I could think to do – I got into line.

By the time I got up to order, most of the people were back to their own business. By San Francisco standards, I was nowhere near an odd enough scene to warrant further attention. At least from the patrons. "Flowers and coffee? You must be in deep shit or you're the Holy Grail of guys."

She – Tiffany by her nametag – was pretty enough. Red-hair with a speckle of freckles and a bright smile. While she completely missed hitting the nail on the head, her words definitely inflated the ego. Holy Grail was a compliment that was completely unexpected. But at the same time, I could tell that she was sizing me up, and hoping that somehow I was there for her. Knowing that I should have headed out the moment I saw Cari wasn't here was starting to become obvious. She was probably working at the Starbucks on Powell Street and I was going to miss her shift, knowing my luck.

"I'm looking for Cari." Yea, she was definitely hoping to have a secret admirer. "She told me that she worked at the Starbucks downtown and I forgot which one she said." That wasn't completely true but it made me sound less like a stalker. I wish Cari had told me so I didn't feel like such a fool, and getting hushed remarks about holding up the line. "I see she's not here. Can you maybe tell me when she'll be in or give me her number so I can tell her I got something for her?" I lifted the flowers a little so that it was obvious and not some sleazy pick-up line.

All Tiffany gave me was a blank stare. Maybe she saw the holes in what I said. If I was looking for her and not just calling her, then maybe I was a stalker or a crazy ex-boyfriend that she changed her number to avoid.

"There's no Cari's that work here, but I'll take you up on whatever you had planned for her." Tiffany seemed to have recovered. Only problem was that it made it so much harder to talk to her and still find out something about where Cari was working. Maybe there was some Starbucks employee database Tiffany could crack into like a phonebook.

Then again, if there was some phonebook, I could risk what would happen now and take another chance at the one on Powell. Maybe I'd get someone a little more sympathetic like a girl who'd appreciate the grand gesture I was trying to pull off or a guy willing to give me a break.

"It's a tempting offer, but Cari's the only girl for me. She stole my heart and I want to make sure mine is the last one she wants to take." I couldn't stop the smile growing on my face. Yea, that's exactly what I want. I want to be her last one. "Thanks for your help, Tiffany, but I should be going. I need to find her."

I didn't wait for a snappy response. It wasn't hard to imagine one would be flying my way after turning her down, especially in a busy coffee shop mid-morning. At least I could still make it to the other one and see Cari before it was too late. I didn't want to have to wait another day to see her and hold her again.

I'm not sure what I expected out of a cabaret. There was no backdoor entrance or secret password to get inside. No seedy clientele with a huge bald bouncer. There was just a perky teenage girl behind the glass window selling tickets in the dated theatre. It threw me back to my first movie experience as a kid seeing *The Lion King* with my father in the lighted, glitzy two-screen magical place that was our town theatre.

The inside had that old-time glamour. Instead of movie posters on the walls, there were old bills of past shows, even a few vintage burlesque signs. Instead of rows of seats, tables dotted the floor and a few booths stood in the back, facing the stage. The stage crew was going a quick clean-up of what looked like all the glitter that once populated the craft aisle of a department store. I could only imagine why gallons of glitter were needed and the running tab when there were shows five nights a week. It seemed the first few tables by the stage were covered in the stuff and were best to be avoided. Then again, didn't I want Cari to see me? She had invited me once months ago. I had no idea what to expect here and maybe it was best to stick to the shadows of the back. It would definitely be better to be able to see any boyfriend rushing the stage to congratulate her on a good performance. I knew that's what I'd do if she was mine.

Sitting near the back did afford me a good view of the whole stage. I wondered what the show would be like. Did Cari still dance? Was she part of a group... with the men in thongs? How far did she go in taking it off?

The lights dimmed, almost engulfing the room in darkness. Each table felt like its own little world with a sole candle in the center that gave away the outline of a body watching.

"Ladies and gentlemen, welcome to Andros Theatre. Please direct your attention to the stage and silence everything else but your hands as our own C Troupe welcomes you to the show!"

Music started as the curtain rose. Five shadowed bodies. As the stage lights turned a rosy hue, three men and two women in firefighter ensembles faced away from the audience. Actually, it looked like the women were dressed more like fire instead of fighters. There was a blonde but, when she turned around, it was clear that she wasn't Cari. The odds that she didn't dance anymore just doubled against me. What was the point in staying? This was the last place that I figured Cari would be and, short of stalking the Promenade every day, I was never going to find her. I just paid twenty bucks on a hunch. Then again that was nothing compared to the scheme to fly out here to win her back.

People around me were cheering for something on stage. Two loud pops drew my attention in time to see blue confetti shoot out of the two cannons sported by... men in thongs. When the last drifted to the floor, the women were now in blue thongs and, oh my god, blue water drop pasties with smiley faces. They took a bow as the lights dimmed.

I had zoned out for the show, but holy hell that finish. Sure it left little to the imagination, for both the women and the men. Maybe it wasn't a complete waste of twenty bucks. Maybe some ogling would be exactly what I needed to forget Cari.

Fat chance.

A few people got up and walked around, only to return minutes later with a snack. That popcorn smelled good. I started to get up when the next act came on. Maybe it was out of habit to sit and wait for intermission after being in a movie theatre enough times, or it could have been what the announcer said. But I sat down so as not to disturb the others around me... and so not to draw attention from her.

"Now, ladies and gents, give it up for the star of the troupe.... Crr-yss-taal Cari!"

The lights raised a light blue. The confetti I thought they cleared had only been rearranged and accented the new piles of white on the stage. The lights danced back in a shimmering effect. It wasn't hard to imagine the winterscape. And damn, I loved winter now.

Her blonde hair had grown and slinked over her shoulder in a messy braid that was perfect. Small shimmers reflected over the locks that matched her soft snow-bunny blue lips and frosty eyelashes. They drifted around the room as someone caused a soft snowfall. Her wandering gaze hesitated a moment and my heart rabbited, thinking she had spotted me, but nothing read on her face.

I watched her near-sheer snowy white dress flutter around her body as she moved to the slow music that had started up. It was so soft that I barely realized when it had started. The fact was that I was so engrossed in Cari's performance. The few strands of golden locks that had fallen free moved with her was a flashback to the sunset hues as she danced between my sheets. I had been the reason those strands had gotten free, and I had tucked them back into place as she rested in my arms.

Her dress dropped and my pants rose. A pale blue laced satin slip fell mid-thigh. And holy fuzzy garter. Memories of those amazing legs wrapped around me flooded back as I watched that thin sliver around that beautiful sun-kissed skin move. It was like we were back in bed and this show was all for me. It felt so intimate and the way her eyes sought out mine amongst the shadows.

"God, Cari." Nothing but a whisper on my lips, lost in the soft music and falling snow.

The satin flowed over her skin as she moved about her snowy world. The slip rose up to her hip, leaving a glimpse of fur. How much did that fuzzy nonsense cover? She turned her back to us and gave a cheeky, seductive look over her shoulder as the pale blue lifted off her skin to pile in the snow.

Cari was practically nude. The tuffs of fur on her hips were only hints that she tried to pass this off for a thong. My mouth watered, remembering the taste of her skin. She didn't need to turn around for me to see those perfect, soft mounds. The little noises she had made when... Shit! No, she couldn't turn around! Panic rose as she started to turn. I didn't want to share anymore of her. I'd pluck out every other eye in the room if it stopped them from getting my memories.

Something round moved just off stage in my peripheral. It wasn't until Cari's gaze tore away towards it did anyone realize out that it was a snowman. Wiggling his branchy fingers, the snow falling increased. In a flash, the snowman charged her. Every instinct I had made me want to barrel up there and into the man.

Overprotective.

I couldn't focus on what was happening. The next thing I knew was that Cari's cute ass was wiggling a little victory dance and the snowman was nowhere to be seen. She didn't seem to have realized the fact that the snowman stole her thong, and let down her hair to rest in soft curls down her back.

She *giggled!*

She giggled and covered those cheeks with one of the snowy pom-poms she suddenly had. The other covered her chest as the snow softened and the lights dimmed to transform Cari into shadows.

I stood standing. I was the only one until someone started to clap and others joined my "standing ovation". At least I hope that was entirely on the fact that I was standing and nothing related to my friend waving hello from my pants.

I had to find her. Now.

Four shadows had returned to clean off the stage. It didn't take a second glance to tell that Cari wasn't one of the silhouettes. Somewhere, there was a beautiful body being covered up. In my mind, I was the one to have stripped her down and I had to see it through to the happy ending.

There was nothing but Tickets and Concessions outside this room with the stage and tables. Somewhere off in the back had to be the dressing rooms. At least that's what all the movies and shows portrayed. That was what my plan was. All the time I was sneaking around, there was the fear of a bouncer lurking or someone throwing me out before I got the chance to see and talk to her. I had to be close to finding her but when it turned silent, I checked my watch. It had been an hour since I slipped out of the show. There was no way Cari was still here. I had managed to find her and come so close only to fail. Or was it that she saw me and had purposely disappeared again? Apart from returning each night, there was no way I could find her; no way I could figure out what happened to us; no way I could get her back. The place was empty and dead silent as I weaved my way to the front and hit the street.

The Haight.

Endless opportunities, but none that would help me find Cari. None, except... if she was still dancing, then maybe her group still went to Greg's. Cari had told me that her group had frequented there. Hell, that place changed its name for them. Now just to find it. Cari had taken us a different way and I didn't know this town as well as her. I could tell the neighborhoods and bridges apart. Maybe if I could find Geary then I could follow it back to the areas I really knew. Or I could just hail a cab and get there before she disappeared on me again.

The neon ice cream cone shown bright as the cab pulled up. I'd walk in and sit beside her. She'll want to explain and tell me how much she missed me. She'll tell me she loves me.

My hand froze on the door. Cari was inside. She was laughing with her group. A guy had his arm around the back of her chair. *She has a boyfriend.* Of course she would. Who could resist someone like Cari? Had they been together all along? She didn't seem the type of person to cheat with a summer fling. The way he sat close and made her smile. The fact that there was something between them. It was damn near hard to miss. It was probably best that things ended how and when they did. It was ridiculous to actually think we had anything after only a week. I shouldn't be here. I only met her because I was on the run and maybe, now, I was just running from Hannah.

I was about leave when the guy next to her pointed my way. I wish Cari's face didn't drop. At least she still recognized me. I should be a little happy about that. She leaned in to whisper in the guy's ear and I knew I shouldn't be here. There was no "what if" to keep me dueling over the idea of going inside. I could walk away. No harm; no foul. But how had that guy crossed the shop without me realizing it? Was I so conflicted over the idea of walking away from Cari and writing her out of my life that I hadn't noticed him walking over? I could run, but would he chase me down? I was staring at, and basically stalking, his girl.

"Hey. You want to come join us?"

That wasn't even in my top twenty responses that I expected to come out of his mouth. He wanted me to join them? Maybe it would make sense if they were gangsters and he wanted to let the others in on my beating. But this was a family-friendly establishment. It even said so on the door. I couldn't imagine this going well, and the look Cari was sending my way didn't dissuade that. The guy dragged over another chair, sitting backwards. That left the recently vacant seat next to Cari. Right next to her boyfriend whom was staring at me between him and his girl.

"So how'd you know Cari?" A girl with glitter still on her face asked as I reluctantly sat down. There wasn't even that Shimmy or Slappy or Silly Sam guy here to make it tolerable. I couldn't spot any waiter or waitress around to rescue me if this went bad.

I hoped that Cari might speak up. She had to know that there were so many wrong ways that I could answer that simple question. I was the guy she had sex with and ran out on. I was that random tourist that picked her up in a bar. I was the guy she cheated on her boyfriend with. None of them felt good saying and I fell back to a tolerable truth.

"We met over the summer." They were all watching me eagerly. All except Cari, whom poked around her sundae. Was she really not going to acknowledge me? "She invited me to one of the shows, but I had to leave for school. I managed to make it to the show tonight. You all were great." That finally seemed to get her attention. She finally looked at me.

"Wait... is your name Jack?" Glitter was just full of questions. When I nodded, she squealed. "Oh. My. God! Jack as in *the* Jack?"

How does one answer that? I have no idea if that's a good thing or not. If her friend knew me, Cari must have said something. Could it be that I nearly died running? Had food on my face? Was a horrible kisser? Sucked in bed?

I was going to answer but Glitter wasn't looking at me. Her gaze was set on a blushing Cari. Her ravenous smile grew. "It is!"

Cari tried to hide behind her bowl of ice cream and I couldn't blame her. I wanted to disappear too. Not only was her friend way too excited over this revelation, but Cari's boyfriend was staring a hole in the side of my head.

"I'm sure it wasn't exactly like Cari told you. We were just friends and she showed me around town."

It was all for the benefit of her boyfriend. I had no idea what Cari really told him, but I had to dissuade him from finding a reason to come after me. This was probably something Cari never imagined happening, and I didn't really want to drive a wedge in her relationship.

"So you're not the hot guy that Cari seduced and then ran out on, only then to mope around for weeks?" Her boyfriend had leaned in and was too close. Shit, he really did know. Cari probably wanted to come clean and told him. They probably had worked it out... until now. "I doubt she'd have come up with that whole snow routine if you were just friends."

Ugh, her boyfriend was annoying with his air quotes around "just friends". We weren't just friends and it seemed like he was trying to provoke me into admitting it. I couldn't help but look to Cari with the little admission that her routine was for me. That was probably enough of owning to being the Jack that had caused such a scandal.

"Cari, you're in some deep shit now." Wait, what? Her boyfriend was laughing. What was happening? Had I fallen asleep at the cabaret and this was my own twisted dream of finding her?

She reached behind me to smack the guy's arm. "Shut up, Todd, or I'll tell mom that her darling son likes to shake it in a sparkly purple thong." Snickers erupted around the table. Um, okay... maybe it wasn't a boyfriend. Sounded more like a threat to invoke an attack from an in-law. But Cari didn't wear a wedding ring. It still didn't make sense to me.

Glitter leaned over. "Todd is Cari's brother, and obviously they love each other," she laughed.

Brother? I guess that could explain things too. "You told your brother about me?" I was back to staring at Cari, confused. Why would she do that?

"Yea, well." Cari was trying to avoid answering me. I was almost certain that if she didn't, someone at this table would. "He just wanted to know what I was up to. Like a description and name he could give the cops if you turned out to be an axe murderer."

There was a pause, then we both busted out laughing. That was the most ridiculous thing that I ever heard. It was clear to the two of us that I wasn't close to being an axe murderer, but I could see how her brother could imagine such a thing. Cari probably teased him by distorting things too. That was what siblings did, right?

I leaned my elbows on the table. A quick glance at Cari and I knew it was my turn to have a little fun. "So what has Cari said about me?" I could tell Glitter was torn between dishing out the dirty details and keeping her loyalties in check. "I got some things I could tell you about her in exchange."

Her brother laughed and clapped me on the back. "Cari, I like him." Todd's approval meant little to me when those feisty blue eyes were turned my way.

"And what kind of things you got on me?" She asked, avoiding looking at me.

Her tone seemed to suggest that she thought I was going to kiss-and-tell. After contemplating mass murder at her show and now sitting with her brother and friends, those details were forever mine alone. It was tempting to let her squirm a little. Then again, I don't really want to start off on the wrong foot. It looked that she was giving me a second chance; I shouldn't push for a third.

"Well, you finally asked me out and brought me here to only steal my ice cream." That elicited a few snickers and a dignified "I did not!" from Cari.

"The ice cream thief strikes again!" It was a little odd to have someone kind of rooting on my side, especially her brother. "Looks like you owe him, sis."

I was pretty sure there was double meaning there. The severity of stole ice cream didn't warrant such seriousness. Then again, maybe that was the sibling dynamics. "Well, I'm off for a month this time unless I transfer. There'd be plenty of time, if you want, Cari."

Todd got up to whisper something in her ear. Her expression changed slightly. Her brother must have known they slept together. A nod to the rest of the group and everyone got up. I figured they were all leaving for some rehearsal, or maybe just to do their celebratory tradition away from a tourist party crasher. Of course! I was putting them out. I really just needed Cari's number.

"I can go and –" Her brother's hands pushed me back down into my seat.

"We have to make the run for supplies before the store closes. Cari's got plenty of snow. Just make sure she gets home safe. Alright?"

It took a moment, but I got what he was telling me: *You got her now. Don't let her run off because this is your only shot. Hurt my sister and I'll beat your ass.*

Nodding, I did the only thing I could and went along. It wasn't a bad plan, unless Cari hated what her brother was doing for me. She never stopped glaring at Todd until they disappeared out of the shop.

"So..."

"Are you really here a month?"

Speaking at the same time, we stared at each other, trying to figure out who was going to speak first. I was just trying to break the ice whereas she was actually interrogating me. I nod, in case she was going to try speaking again. I didn't want to talk over her. It didn't feel right to plow through the conversation to where I wanted it to go, even though I had every right after what happened. I still cared too much about Cari to be that rough with her.

"You're really thinking about transferring?" Cari knew my photography major didn't lock me into one place, thousands of miles away. It wasn't pre-med or law at some Ivy League school.

But it also meant not upheaving my life on a whim. "I am if I have a real shot with you."

Cari hid her thoughts and feelings from me when she turned away to poke at her sundae. Damn! I had want to kiss her so bad and now she was driving me crazy by depriving me of those emotions I need to see from her. I just want to make her face me and kiss her senseless. Did she not feel anything for me anymore? Had it been too long?

"I was hoping that I didn't run into you at the theatre." That got her attention. Those ocean gems searched my face, trying to figure out what I was saying. If I didn't know where I was going with this, I would be right alongside her.

This guy didn't want to find me, yet flew across the country and walked into her burlesque show at the only theatre within walking distance of the ice cream shop.

It didn't make sense from her perspective.

"I was hoping that I'd find you at work. I think I might actually have it down pack now. I buy flowers from Kevin on Sutter, head over to Starbucks on Powell. I get my seat by the window and I wait all day for you. I almost have your schedule figured out. After a week, I should; but see, I started first at the other one downtown. I was dressed to the nines to impress you and it was the first time that I bought flowers from Kevin." I almost forgot that she doesn't know who Kevin is. "Oh, he's the guy from the Tenderloin that sells his blooms out of these two big buckets. Nice guy. Has two kids.

"They actually tell their dad what to sell me now. The first day, I bought these tulips that were the color of a sunrise. He had a bunch of roses and Gerber daisies, but those tulips just called out to me. They reminded me of the sky when we went running that day. Somehow, that sunrise had waited just for us." Her expression wasn't something that I knew how to read. I had never been looked at like this before, and I did the only thing that I could think of – I kept talking. The more I talked, the more she had to stay.

"What was today's flower?" Her voice was so quiet that, if I didn't see her lips moving, I wouldn't have known she said anything. At least she wasn't out the door or knocking me for dropping so much on flowers that she'd never get.

It wasn't the flashiest flower, but they had a nice light smell. It was a flower that reminded me of her, and I wondered if Kevin actually knew her. "Lilacs."

Her chair scraps back and Cari's getting up. Shit! It was too much. I put out too much too soon and she was going to walk out that door with my heart again. "Cari, wait."

She freezes and stares back at me. "What?"

I can see how badly she wants to get away. Is there anything I can say to get her to stay?

"I'm just getting a take-out box. I'm not leaving behind my Rockin' Robin."

Was that my hearting beating again?

I want to believe that it was her intent all along to get a container for her relatively untouched sundae. Then again, I remember the size of these bowls and Cari probably ate half of it even though it didn't look that way. But I couldn't. She barely talked to me, much less looked at me since everyone left. And she was still leaving. Getting up, I follow after her but she was already on her way back with the little white box.

"Cari, whatever I said to upset you, I'm sorry. I didn-" Her hand on my mouth silences the words.

"Nothing you said upset me, Jack. It was a lot to take in, yea know?" She takes her hand away from my lips and there's a strange expression that passes over her face. It's gone in a second, before it could be deciphered. "No one's ever bought me flowers, much less every day. It just made me realize that you wouldn't have come out here and done anything but that. I mean, you flew all the way out here for me, Jack. I've dated guys from Oakland that wouldn't even cross a bridge. You crossed the country."

It feels like the next words out of her mouth would be how much she appreciated the gesture but just didn't feel the same. Maybe that was why she couldn't look at me before. Cari was over us and trying not to give me false hope. I have to say something but when I open my mouth she knocks me out.

"If I was brave enough, I would have flown across the country to get you back. I'm pretty sure that I fell in love with you last summer and I know that I never fell out."

I want to kiss her so bad. At least she's looking at me and I can see how much she'd wants me to do just that. Her eyes drift down to my lips for a moment and I wonder if she'll make the first move.

My lips claim hers before she can look away from them. I pull her close and can feel her hand on the back of my neck, holding on and making this real. Catcalls start erupting but neither of us cares enough to stop. Only when we're out of breath with kiss-swollen lips does she pull back an inch.

"Let me walk you home."

Those bright eyes look up at me. Could she have thought anything else of me? Not only could I physically not let her go, but I couldn't let her leave me now. I knew how she felt and I proved how deep my emotions ran. If nothing else, I'd be able to steal another kiss after saying goodnight to her at the door.

Slowly, Cari nods. She turns to leave but stops after a step, looking conflicted and confused. She goes back to toss the take-out box on the table. "Forget it."

She takes my arm before leading me out the door. The cheers were loud enough to still hear once we stepped outside. She didn't stop walking. Maybe the catcalls had gotten to her. Being away for so long made her harder to read. I thought I knew what she was thinking, but I doubted myself.

"Cari, are you okay? Wanna talk about it?" She was walking a little too determined away from the ice cream shop, and dragging me along.

"I'm sorry." Cari slows to a more normal pace beside me. "I just want to get home."

My heart drops and my feet stop. She was running away from me. But why was she taking me along for the ride? I was I just her security blanket on the street because it was night? Even if that's all I was to her, I wasn't going to stop and abandon her like my mind was screaming at me to do. She was leading me on and I was going to end up battered and bruised after tonight.

"Jack, I want to go home." Cari stood in front of me. "Do you know why?"

To get rid of me?

I shake my head, feinting ignorance to the truth, and she continues. "I want you to see my place. I want to invite you in for a cup of coffee before I lose my nerve. God, after that kiss," she must have read all my hesitation, "Jack, I want to do things to you that I can't get away with doing in a family-friendly ice cream shop.

Not to mention the embarrassing sundae they'll name after us."

Her hand comes up to rest against my cheek. Her thumb gently paces back and forth. "Would you like to come up for a cup of coffee?"

Chapter Twelve

I look around her place and it's not exactly what I expected. Her walls are rather bare, but what is on them speaks volumes. They're nature shots. An enlarged purple Gerber daisy photograph is the first one that I spot that draws me into her apartment. The few others, wooden trails and waterway could be of anywhere, but the Golden Gate and street markets give it away that all of these photographs are local. I want to see something of mine up on her walls. I want to give her something worthy of being nailed up to the partial brick walls.

My eyes are drawn next to the bay window with its plush seat cushion. The color reminds me so much of Cari's eyes. On the wall next to it is a tall bookcase, and the closer I get the more I see. I could spot Tennyson from across the room, but I didn't realize the frames dotting the shelves were of her and her family. I want to know more. I want to know who they all are and what made them laugh in that one or where they were in another. I spot her brother in a couple, but he's the only one I can pick out besides Cari. A giggle finally pulls my eyes away.

"Is something funny?"

Obviously it is, but it makes her laugh even more as she walks over with two coffee cups. I had thought she was joking about the coffee, but obviously that was a legit part of getting me back to her place. I thank her as I take one from her and get a taste. Either she spied on me or Cari got lucky. Well, I was sure she'd get lucky later.

"I've just been watching you scope out my place. It was amusing to see you wandering around." She took a sip. Her eyes were full of mischief as she watched me over the top of her cup. "You look so interested."

"That's because I am." There's no point to hide the truth. "I've always wanted to get to know you, Cari. Seeing your place, I never would have guessed some of these things about you." I nod towards the bookcase. On the top are a couple antique metal perpetual motion toys. "Either you like collecting old stuff or secretly nerd out for engineers."

She laughs. "Old stuff? Wow, Jack." She shakes her head, but it's because she's speechless. "You could call them antiques or collectables or thrifty treasures. And I don't nerd out." That was probably true. Nothing else in the living room was proof to that statement. "I've always wanted one of those birds that bob back and forth, pretending to take a sip of water. I saw this one at one of the booths during the summer flea market and picked him up. George very much likes his home up there."

"George?"

Cari said it so matter-of-factly that I can't not laugh. Is she serious? I hope not because I couldn't stand it if she got any more adorable.

It earns me a light punch on the arm. "What's wrong with George? Better than stinky ole Jack."

Oh, this was how she was going to play?

I set my cup on her coffee table before trapping her in my arms. "I'm stinky now? Here I thought you liked me," I tease. "Just wanted to bring me back here and make fun of me, huh?" I want to tickle her. It's just the cheating little kid in me. But it's an urge that could get me splashed with burning hot coffee.

"Yes. You're stinky and smelly and-" My lips cut her off.

I've tried to resist her all night, but I can't anymore. Cari's too much for me to fight and, now that I know this side of her, I can't not be all in. If she breaks my heart again, I'll have to deal with it then. Because there's nothing that is going to stop me from giving us another chance.

Her lips move against mine before she pulls back. It's not enough. I want more and I try to steal another, but Cari's taking a step back. Her eyes lock onto mine as she leans down to put her coffee cup beside mine. She's leading me upstairs, with her hand in mine as soon as the danger of hot liquids is handled. Cari hasn't said a word, but I see it in those beautiful eyes.

We pass a bathroom and a closed door that I'd guess would be a closet, but my gaze zeroes in on the other door. The door open... with a bed. I don't get a chance to look around this room. I don't want to. I know everything that I need to – Cari's here.

She is trying to pull me into bed with her, but that's just not going to happen. I stop her with one knee on the bed and a confused look on her face. "Jack, what's wrong?"

Is this not what you want?

The tenting in my pants is evidence enough to that. It's just that I know I've done everything right by her and it feels like I still have so much to make up to her, but that's not what's important. We're only going to have this one moment. This one moment where she's going to think back later and decide if she regrets me walking back into her life or if that summer we had was the best it would ever be between us. And I don't want her to regret. I don't want her to think. I want her to feel it inside. I want her to know how right this is and how perfect we are together. I want her to know how much I love her, and to truly believe that and believe in what we can have.

I want to worship her and that's why I can't let her drag me to bed.

"Come here," I say softly. For the first time tonight, she seems a bit hesitant. Maybe it's because it looks like I'm doing the opposite of making love to her. I kiss her forehead as my arms wrap around her body and sneak up the back of her shirt to that warm sun-kissed skin. "Nothing's wrong. I just want to do things right by you. I don't want to you wake up and not know how much I love you. I don't want you to feel like I've come back just to use you tonight or to string you along before I leave."

"Jack, what are you talking about? You haven't done anything like that."

Oh, but I had. I let her go and then I dated someone else. I wasted all that time when I could have been here with her. I could have been with her and not failed her like boyfriends of the past. I could have been here proving I deserved the chance she gave me, that I deserved her. There was so much that I didn't do that I should have.

"I want you to want me, and not just for tonight. I want to stick by your side, even if you try to kill me with another run. I want to be your boyfriend. I want to the last guy to ever have you."

Her lips parted slightly with that last confession. Did Cari think I was about to propose? I guess it really sounded like that was what was coming. The intention had just been to tell her that I was planning to stick around until we both died. Preferably all *The Notebook* style – at the same time because neither of us could live without the other. Yea, I'd admit that I saw that movie. Guess having another relationship while waiting for the one that held my heart might not have been completely pointless.

"Cari, my future is out here with you. That's all I'm saying right now. All I want is to be with you. It's all I've ever wanted. I want to make sure that you don't regret me, and that you fall completely and madly in love with me." And have my babies... which I couldn't sanely add. Guess my mother's nagging was getting to me, or maybe that's really what I was thinking about when I looked at Cari. She was my everything.

The last thing I wanted to do was make her cry and I could tell that my words had gotten to her. Maybe it was too much to assume that neither of us had really changed from that week together. Even if her brother made her out to be single, maybe it wasn't a relationship that she wanted. Maybe asking for one was too much, but the cards had to get put on the table now before it was too late. The ball was really in Cari's court. When she leaned in to kiss me, it left that worrying voice behind.

Her hands crept under my shirt and I let her lift it up off me. It granted me a moment to read her face, or try to, and I saw the same way I was feeling. Everything I said was what Cari wanted me to hear from her.

I lifted her up against me and carried her the few steps to lay her down on the bed. My hands worked on getting those pants off as my lips got another taste of her. I worked them down enough to be able to slip a hand between her thighs. Cari didn't gasp like the last time. Instead her body rocked up against my hand. Her tongue slipped into my mouth and I slipped inside her with another digit. I wanted to put myself right back inside that sweet warmth. I wanted to, but I... I wasn't sure why I was hesitating when I knew Cari was ready.

Cari was ready alright.

She pushed me over onto my back and straddled me before I could realize what she was doing. Her hands had pushed down my jeans and boxers enough to allow my straining erection to pop up free. In the tussle, she had kicked her legs free and now had me trapped. And when my hands went to her waist, Cari grabbed my wrists and pinned them over my head. I'd be lying if I said that didn't turn me on even more.

"Cari," I begged. She cut me off with her mouth before I could even grovel more. I wanted to beg her to just grind against me a little higher so – that by the grace of god and all that's good – that my tip would get an inch. All it would take then would be a thrust of the hips to finally be inside her, but she seemed to realize that.

She lifted her hips up and used her ass to push back my cock. It slid into the groove between her cheeks and I realized too late how evil Cari was. I could feel her smirking as she kissed me and how her grip tightened on my wrists when I tried to budge.

"You want me, Jack?" Oh, god, she had no idea. "Beg."

What did she think I'd been doing? I started to speak and she kissed me. I tried to move my hands and she held on tighter. How else could I beg? What did she want? To torture me? To take everything away? It was emotionally painful not being inside her but now it was getting physically painful. I had tried to sneak my way in but Cari denied me at every turn. My cock throbbed for her. My balls ached, wanting to release. I struggled to think straight. Maybe she just wanted me to put on a show. Well, then, I was going to disappoint her. I couldn't do anything right now. I just had to wait and pray she gave me herself. And maybe that was it – to beg by giving up control. That seemed how Cari wanted to play. It was worth a shot.

I relaxed my arms and tried, against my better judgement, to not to rock my hips against her. I couldn't control my cock though. It throbbed and twitched just from touching her soft skin alone. I just stared up at her face, framed by those golden locks. I wanted to at least kiss her, but I needed to play along. If this wasn't what she wanted by begging, then I was taking that kiss.

"Do you think this is begging?" She was intently watching me. Cari rocked her hips against me and I almost lost my control. "It seems like you're given up instead, Jack."

So this was wrong? Cari didn't want me to be submissive? This wasn't begging by being passive and letting her decide what happens? I wasn't a slave waiting for a master's command? My silence wasn't willing her to...?

Her lips moved against mine while her hips worked me along her ass. I was so confused, but I wasn't going to complain. I played the game she wanted. Maybe it was begging in and of itself just because I was going to do whatever she wanted. And Cari finally gave me what I wanted.

She sank down on me slowly and I felt my balls tighten up. There was no way I could let myself come just from anticipation. I wasn't going to blow things two seconds in... but, god, did Cari feel more amazing than I remembered! At this point, she had me. My whole body gave into her every whim, and it was awesome.

Her hips ground against me and brought me just a little deeper. But I wanted more. I wanted her to ride me harder. I wanted her to be writhing in pleasure beneath me. I wanted everything with her. I needed everything with her. I needed more than just a little bit of friction to keep things going.

"Cari, more... please." Maybe I had to beg. Maybe she didn't know just how much I needed it.

She leaned down to kiss my neck, not once changing the rhythm of her hips. "I waited so long, Jack. Just a little more."

A little more of what? I did not know. Cari kissed along my jawline until she got to my ear and then the little minx gave me a play-bite. I had never expected this side to come out of Cari. It had me... pleasantly confused. It was just a chance for her to be her and, hell, if it wasn't hot.

Then her ass started to bounce.

My eyes rolled into the back of my head as Cari twerked on top of me. It was grinding and a whole lot of something else. It felt like she somehow was working the whole of me. She got my balls bouncing with every move she made, and she was working my head quickly towards what was going to make me blow. It felt so amazing that I almost didn't care if I gave in because she knew this was forever now.

And just like that, she stopped.

My eyes cracked open to see her head thrown back and eyes closed as she slowed back to the old grind. She just took my breath away. Then her eyes drifted open and found mine. Those ocean orbs had a spark in them that I'd never saw before. And it was gone a second later when her lips claimed mine.

Cari had me. As her lips whispered promises, her body stole me forever. Her body fluttered and held onto me, taking everything I had.

"Mhmm."

Something warm pressed back against me. It was so soft and warm. I just wanted to pull my body closer and burying myself deep in whatever it was. It was until that something started rubbing against my groin. It was quickly getting me... more awake.

"Mhmm, Jack."

I freeze. I'm wide awake now. All I see is a blonde mess of hair on the pillow beside me and I have no idea where I am. I do know that, whether this girl is meaning to or not, her ass is doing all the right things to put us in the situation we evidently we were in last night. Which doesn't make much sense to me. I'm a free man, but my cock never really wanted anyone since Cari. Irrationally, I know I've cheated on her. It's been months and I might never find her again, but I fucking screwed up and cheated.

She pushes back against me and my cock slips between her thighs. Fuck! I have to get it out of there before I make everything worse. I promised myself there'd be no one else until things were settled with Cari. I needed to see things through before giving myself an honest shot at moving on. I need... Cari?

I watch as a hand brushes back the locks of gold from her face and trails slowly down her body. The hand disappears down her front as it reaches her hip and my mind's going all kinds of dirty places right now. I bet her hand is rubbing the aching spot between her thighs and that her hips are going to start rocking. She'll slip one finger inside, just to test the waters and moan a little.

She'll turn herself on and start thrusting into herself to try and reach that spot that got her coming hard on my cock.

I'm growing harder between her thighs just thinking about it. I can feel her starting to get wet, but I can't feel what her hand's doing to herself. Cari's moaning, but it's not at what I thought she was doing. I flinch when her cold hands touch me. It feels like fire licking ice, and it feels so good. My hips rock against her and pump me into her hand as much as her ass will allow.

"Let me in, sweetheart," I beg. I'm loving this torture but I need her. I fucking need her bad. Her ass just pushes back to tease me. Ugh, it's frustrating not to just be given what I want. I could take it, or I could give her a taste of her own medicine.

I snake my hand down over her hip. Her body reacts instantly when my finger flicks across her clit. It's enough of a shock to get her jerking my cock, but Cari doesn't give any indication of letting me in.

If that's the game she wants to play...

My finger flicks across that sensitive bud before slicking itself in her wetness and making a round before slipping inside. Her head falls back against my chest, her eyes closed while her hand explores the feel of me. I start off gentle and slow after last night, finding an easy rhythm. Her hand matches mine. I sink in deeper and she gives my cock a light squeeze with every pump. The heel of my palm rubs against her clit and her hips rock back against me, teasing the part she can't reach.

She was going to get us both off if she kept this up.

I wrap my free arm around her, limiting what she could do to me. My hand buried inside her pumps faster. She gives up all attempt to get me off for a moment. She gives in completely... and then her hand frantically tries to get me off. I can feel her body already tensing up. I was going to win, but now I want to get her off first. She was already getting me close.

"Jack," she whined.

Following her lead last night, I kissed her neck and nibbled along the way. Cari didn't let up, so I didn't either. I heard her moan as I leaked into her hand. That got her off. Her thighs clamped tight on my hand. She trapped my cock as well, just as I came all over her golden thighs. By the time I was spent, Cari had gone lax enough to restore circulation to my hand, and cock.

"I love you, Jack," she whispered.

Those four words weren't something that I expected to hear so soon from her. I expected that she'd want to be in a relationship with me and work our way back to those feelings. Maybe it had been foolish on my part to believe that. I just knew that it made my heart skip a beat to hear that she loved me.

"I love you too." It was the cliché response, but it was the truth.

My hand drifted up from her thighs and wrapped around her waist. Just waking up to hold her would have been enough to make this a good day, but Cari had made this a great day. It left the bar pretty high on how I was going to make good on my word to do right by her.

"After we get cleaned up, let's go out for breakfast."

Her eyes closed as she leaned back into me. Cari was probably contemplating it. Going out meant getting dressed and actually having to function today. It meant that we probably couldn't talk about what happened between us last night or this morning. Not that there really was anything to talk about. Our feelings seemed pretty clear. I just needed to hear her say that she was mine.

Cari nodded, and then I asked her. "There's no one else I'd ever want to be with."

That was all I needed to hear.

Chapter Thirteen

Cari sat curled up in the bay window of her apartment. Her gaze was fixated on the phone in her hands. Her brother had texted her yesterday that there were new reviews of the burlesque show online. It had her glued to the screen when she wasn't asking me to confirm or deny the comments. For the most part, the reviews were great.

I was glad that she was getting the recognition but now that I was her boyfriend – officially – I didn't like knowing other men were looking at her. It was probably something I was going to deal with for a long time. I couldn't ask her to stop doing what she loved. At least I could be happy that I was the one she was always coming home to.

"I'm moving George." My hand reached for the bird.

"Don't you dare!"

Car glared at me. She knew I had it out for the bird since the day she brought me home from the cabaret. I thought it was silly, but my attempts to get rid of it now were just to get a rise out of her. She looked adorable and downright sexy when that fire got in her eye.

"But where would I put my priceless..." I rummaged in the box of my stuff. "... Train CD?"

I went to push the drinking bird knickknack aside. I don't think I've ever seen Cari move that fast. Not even on our morning runs. She snatched the beat-up old CD right out of my hands.

"Don't you dare! George deserves a place of honor and this... well, this is something you can just toss on the table." She backed away and started to toss it on the coffee table but stopped. "Wait. Why didn't you just put this on your computer and throw it away?" Cari flipped it over in her hand. "Does anyone even listen to these guys anymore? I thought they were all like dead."

I couldn't help but laugh. Train wasn't dead. They just were... different. The CD had been a relic of Ava's but it didn't have the same hold over me as it once did. It was just another item in my junk box that my mom shipped out to me. Maybe it was in there as a reminder of what was back home and an attempt to make me homesick to bring me back. While she had heard about Cari now and then, I don't think she really liked that her grown son was moving across the country for a woman, and for college.

"Fine, George can stay." I carry my box of stuff and set it in the corner. "For now," I tease, under my breath. I know she heard me because Cari huffed and started mumbling something on her way back to her perch in the window.

The sound of the mail slot door clinking got my attention. I nudged the box squarely in the corner with my foot before walking across the room to get the mail. There wasn't a rush except that I notice there were a few pieces of mail still stuck in the slot.

"We got a lot of mail today," I said, bending over to retrieve the pile of envelopes.

I filtered through the stack as I made my way back to the couch and plopped down on the end closest to Cari. The daily newspaper was tossed onto the coffee table, along with the couple magazines. I'd flip through the photography one later while Cari read up on the latest celebrity gossip and 101 ways she should please a man or change me or about the new "it" sex positions. If she didn't get ideas from the fashion bits for her burlesque shows, I'd have thrown out that stupid magazine. I knew she didn't need some stupid list to please me nor did she need to add anything to spice up life in the bedroom... and she didn't need to change me because I was perfect. I hope.

"Huh." I set down the mail into two stacks – hers and the unfiltered bunch. Besides the magazine I subscribed to and the junk mail, everything was Cari's. But this thick envelope had my name on it in fancy print.

I recognized the return address listed in the corner, but what was Connor sending me? We had just hung out a couple weeks ago when I took Cari home for a visit and to meet my parents. He should have given me anything he meant to mail then. My finger slipped under the flap and tore open the top of the envelope. The paper inside was just as thick and fancy as the outside.

So it was decided then.

I leaned my head back over the armrest to look at Cari. "Just got Connor's invitation to the wedding. Seems he and Lisa finally set a date. Wanna be my "plus one"?"

"Well," Cari drew out the word. I could the smile she was trying to hide. "I guess I could deal with your terrible dancing and free cake."

There's something about weddings that really makes you think about what you're doing with your life. I'm sure that if I wasn't here with the most beautiful girl in the world that I'd be wondering about some really big things my life was missing. Instead of mulling over my lackluster existence, I'm watching the love of my life laughing and smiling with my friends. As if Cari could make me love her more.

"So when you gonna put a ring on that?"

Connor sidles up next to me at the cake table. What can I say? The tower of girly fondant flowers really called out to my sweet tooth for a second piece. Sure, it put me in perfect view of those blue eyes and sun-kissed legs... I'm totally just standing here for the now half-eaten cake on my plate.

"You want me to propose at your wedding, Con?" I glance his way, making a show of rolling my eyes. But the look on his face says exactly that. I should propose now. But there's no way I'm stealing his thunder on his big day.

Connor looks serious though. He knows I've been dragging my feet, but things between Cari and I don't need a piece of paper to make it legit. We live together.

Our lives are together. She's practically my wife. And yet, I'm hesitating for some stupid reason. God, I wish I knew why. Connor's already told me it's because of Ava. It feels wrong to say it out loud, but I don't think about her anymore. I don't know; maybe I am still supposed to be thinking about her. It's not like there's an Appendix B in some life manual that I can flip to for situations like this. I just decided to focus on my future and getting there instead.

And the only future I want is Cari.

Somehow, with her, I was getting more than forever.

Epilogue

I never thought that I would find the love of my life. Especially not at this point in my life. I had been so sure that it was Ava and then Cari. But his girl beat them all by a mile.

"Ella Noel Havest," I couldn't help smiling at her, "you are coming home with me."

"Oh, no you don't, daddy. You bring my little girl back here right now." I had wondered how far I would get. Hospital room door was pretty far.

Beautiful blue eyes stared up at me. "We don't need mommy, right, beautiful?"

"Hey! What am I now? Chop liver?" Cari laughed. "I know you're trying to make me jealous by sweet-talking our daughter. And I hate that it's working."

Hearing her mom, she started to fuss. I sure knew where I stood fast. I gave her back to Cari before walking around the hospital bed and taking up residency again in the recliner. They looked so good together, and being a mom came so naturally to Cari. I watched as she smoothed back Ella's few dark curls before kissing her forehead. Cute little murmurs bubbled up out of the little pink blanket.

I watched as Cari adjusted herself to give our sweet pea lunch. "Now who's making whom jealous?" She just rolled her eyes and shook her head. At least she was back to her good mood after such a long labor. "Ella, you better know that you're only borrowing those. Those are daddy's and he's going to want them back."

"I can't believe you right now," she laughed. "You really are lecturing our baby. She's only a day old."

"I know. I just need to lay down some ground rules. Like all poopy diapers are for mommy and all nap times are for me." I chuckle, seeing her reaction. I know I'd really going to get it when we finally get home. "And she can't wake us up before seven in the morning, no spit-up when I have to burb her, no ear-splitting cries."

Cari's really amused. I doubt it from whatever the baby's doing to her breast. "Jack, you're going to be sorely disappointed then. Did you not read the baby book?" I had. More out of panic than actually wanting to know about mucus and gooey things that were coming out of the baby. When I shrugged, she continued. "Every baby cries and wakes up during the night. Are you sure you really are up for this, Jack?"

Am I up for it? It wouldn't have bothered me if I hadn't seen the flash of fear cross Cari's features. "Cari," I got up and moved to sit on the edge of the bed beside her, "I am sure. I've never been more sure in my life." Leaning over, I kiss her cheek before continuing. "I was sure when I married you and I was sure when we tried for a year. Remember that night I held you in bed and we stayed up all night talking?"

She nodded. We had been trying for almost ten months without even one pregnancy scare, or rather, surprise. Cari had started giving up on having a family. Her brother had gotten serious with someone. The one I used to tease and call Glitter from her troupe had gotten pregnant. She had kept seeing babies and kids everywhere, which wasn't strange when it was summer and everyone was loving the beach. I had tried and promised everything and anything to try and calm her down. I promised a puppy, trying in-vitro, surrogacy, even adoption. Nothing helped, in her mind. I promised that I would never stop trying, that I would never stop making love to her; because, to me, I loved her completely and with my whole heart. I just needed her to be happy. One very long month later, she was late.

"I'm ready to have this amazing family with you. I'm ready to be the best dad that little girl will ever know." Reaching over, I gently brush over Ella's dark curls like mine. Groaning, "It's so hard not to hold her."

I never thought that I would feel this way. Cari, yea. The baby books explained the bond and post-partum, but nothing about the fathers. I never wanted to let go. I never wanted to give her up. I never... Cari kissed my cheek.

"I know, Jack." She must have sensed where my thoughts went. It was so long ago that I found out I was a father. I imagined a little girl with auburn hair and a firecracker personality. I never got to hold her before she was taken from me. Hell, I never got to know that she existed or hear her heartbeat like I had for Ella. Cari knew. She knew that I saw two girls in one. She knew it was hard for me, and she knew that I knew that once our Ella was here that she'd charm the pants off me. Ella sure was making it hard for me to think of anyone else, including myself.

"She's a charmer, just like her mommy." A smile crept on my face. "You warned me this was going to happen and I'm glad I couldn't do anything to stop it." Seemed like Ella didn't want to be forgotten, even for a moment. She was making those cute little noises again.

"Guess someone's full." Cari laughed and cleaned them both up. "Do you want to hold her?"

Did I ever. "Why don't you keep for her a little while? I guess it's technically your turn." Wrapping an arm around her shoulders, I moved closer. "Besides, I can see her better like this." Reaching over, I ran a finger along those soft, tender baby cheeks and got a couple special murmurs from Ella. Those eyes stared up at me and if that didn't make me feel special and loved.

"Ella, we don't need daddy, right? How about we sneak out while he's napping?" She was teasing me. She was teasing me, and she was loving it. I gave her a little squeeze. There was no way I was letting go of either of my girls.

Coming Soon...

The Writer

Chapter One

Adam sat on the bed beside me, leaning against the headboard, while I was sprawled upside down on my stomach. I knew what he was thinking. It was finally Friday night, but this week was hell. It was always hell for me, but Adam got sucked into my brimstone a little more this time. He was the guy dating the freak.

"Hailstorm," he sighed, using my pet name. "It would be so much easier if I was like you. We could get out of this backwards town and just make it, ya know. Just you and me out on our own"

It wasn't anything I hadn't heard before. Adam thought having this... ability was great. It sucked most of the time. I actually had to do hours of research on the simplest homework assignments. I actually had to know shit. Sure, I'd never get a history question wrong on a test... but that's how Genghis Khan accidently had a sex change to be Genny Han: Ruler of the Silken Trail and Murdering Provocateur. That was one mistake that got creative to fix. Who knew blood splatter could make such elegant upholstery for the British Queen? Yes, the royal family had an already bloody history but I accidentally added to the horror of that. There are some fashion choices a girl can just not forget.

With what I could do, there were rules and guidelines. Sure, Adam had seen enough of the reasons why over the five years we've been together. But there were still things I didn't know if he could handle. He'd never be normal again. Trust me, I've tried. Somehow those words meant nothing.

"Haley... Haley... Haley... Haley... Haley..."

Okay, so there was no ignoring him this time. Maybe it was because graduation was coming up and he was worried college would split us if he didn't get into UConn with me. Adam was lucky to get into Northeastern, and it was only a few hours' drive to my second choice school.

"Haley. Haley. Haley. Haley. Haley."

I rolled over onto my back and stared up at his stupid smirking face. I had to give him credit – he knew how to get to me. Adam already had the puppy-dog face ready and it sure made it hard to say no to his baby blues. But that didn't mean I wasn't give in so easily. It might actually be nice having someone else like me around, which always was a thought I had every other time things sucked.

"What?" I laughed.

He just shook his head and sat up to lean over me, his face inches from mine. "Make me like you."

"Okay."

"Please... wait, what?" Those baby blues blinked fast behind the dark hair that fell across his face. He was asking me if I was serious, if I was joking. All I was thinking about was that he needed to cut that mop of hair if he wanted any shot at a summer job this year. Then again I could just make that happen anyways, even though he's said he never wanted me to write about him. He said he was happy earning less as a lifeguard because it let him work on his tan and play hero. I was going to intern at the bank and make a real living this summer.

"Are you serious?" Was I?

I nodded and rolled onto my side when he got off the bed to dig around my backpack for a notebook or some kind of scrap paper. Like he knew that if something wasn't put into my hands soon that I'd back out. But there wasn't much in there anymore with school ending. Just my track uniform and sneakers.

"Adam, there's something you should know." I knew I could have gotten away with going through the motions of writing things out. He would have seen the words on the paper and knew I did my best. He knew that was how it worked and, yet, he would be powerless. "It's going to hurt... a lot." But there was a chance it would work.

He paused in his fruitless search, standing upright. "What ya mean, Hailstorm?"

A superhero name for someone who was not a superhero. It wasn't like I had a great backstory or some sweet way I got this way. What I wouldn't give to have just been bitten by a bug or to have been born like this! The thing was that I really didn't know exactly why this happened to me. I just remembered waking up and being alone. I was the only one able to see my parents after that and they always looked a bit different. Guess that's one of the side effects of being in a fatal car crash – the whole being dead thing. But it was probably just a seven-year-old's mind coping with tragedy to imagine up ghosts existing. I didn't want to make Adam one too.

"I'm this way because of what happened to my parents." Drunk driver. Broad daylight. Three dead, and me in a coma. I was the "oops" baby but I was sure glad to have an older sister, even if she was old enough to be my mom, if she had gotten knocked up by her high school boyfriend. Then again, he was a douche and I'm so glad Jen didn't put out for that weasel.

The bed dipped and it knocked me out of my thoughts. I shouldn't be stuck on the past. It happened and it was over with. It wasn't like I could rewrite it without making things a hundred times worse. And I doubt it was my worried and depressed feelings I was seeing mirrored in Adam's eyes. There was something else on his mind and it seemed like whatever it was had made him, maybe, reconsider.

"Do my parents have to die too?" His voice got quiet at the end and he looked away. It was like he hated himself for wanting this, or maybe he hated me a little for what I paid for it. Not that I had a choice.

It was the first time I heard such regret and pain in his voice. Adam was insanely close to his parents. Even his crazy little kid brother, Ian, that drove him crazy and always seemed to walk in on Adam – naked – in the bathroom. The thought of losing his parents was something Adam wouldn't be able to handle. It was something no one our age should have to even think about. I also wasn't asking him to give up his family. Not if I could write it so he'd never hurt or lose them. I didn't want him to lose his parents either. They kind of because my adoptive parents when Adam and I started dating. Even though I had Jen, there were times when she just wanted to do her own thing and have a life. April and Ken Hathaway were the nicest folks in this town.

Sitting up, I turned his face back towards me. "Hey." His eyes still lingered off to the side. "Buttface, look at me." Okay, there was half of a chuckle. "It's a legit question, but no. I don't think this has anything to do with them." No, what it did have to do with just sucked.

"I don't think they have to be there. I mean, mine were only there because what seven-year-old is allowed to joy ride a Studebaker around Applegate?" Although I probably could have gotten pretty far before my stubby little legs would have needed to hit the brakes. I've gotten lucky before on the drive to school and missed all by one red light through town last week.

"Then what, Hailstorm? How could this hurt me?"

I got both meanings to that question. How could it hurt him when I could write away his pain? The worst part was that I couldn't. That might be part of this whole thing and this wasn't going to happen twice even if Adam wanted it to. How do you explain to the cops that it's just a coincidence to be innocent in two car crashes that happen the exact same way? You can't. Then dating me made it worse if they connected the dots to my parents. Some poor schmuck helping Adam would take the fall over nothing he'd ever done. No, one try was all he was getting, like ever.

"You'd be in a car crash..." Wow, it was hard to face someone and say horrible things. I found my bottom lip between my teeth as I fought how I wanted to break the news. I mean, I didn't really have to tell him everything. Shit, if I didn't love him so much I wouldn't be trying to talk him out of this or even caring if he ended up dead or maimed or a vegetable. Then again, we probably wouldn't be having this talk and I wouldn't be thinking of his battered and bloody body in a hospital bed – cuts all over his face and blood matting his hair; his mother crying at his bedside; his father wanting to kill me for letting this happen.

"Oh." Yea. "How bad?"

Shit. He hadn't given this up. I didn't want to relive all I went through just to tell him exactly how bad it was. I only knew what the pain was like a week later when I woke up. By then I had been in and out of surgery, doped up on pain killers, and healing. But it was still hell.

"Very bad. Remember that time we went skiing and you broke your arm?" Adam nodded. That was a painful experience he'd remember. "It's like that but with every bone in your body broken all at once and then set on fire. Your brain gets bounced around and scrambled so much that just thinking hurts. Nobody tells you that, but they're all begging for you to say something so they know you're alright."

Okay, so there were still bitter memories there. I'd have to tone it down a little and not let it build on my emotions from this week. Adam needed facts. "You'll want to die when you wake up from the coma." Yea, totally leaving out the emotions...

When I finally risked looking at him, his gaze drifted off a little towards my bookcase in the corner. It was hard to read his face to know where his mind was right now. The only worse than a coma was death. Shit was serious.

"Adam, I'll forget this ever came up. Let's go down to Del's and get lemonade."

It was strange that he didn't move. Del's frozen lemonade was the bomb. It was the only thing that made New England tolerable in the summer if you were miles from the beach. Adam was more addicted to the stuff than I was. Yet there was no reaction when I nudged him.

"I want to do this."

Kate Sparrows

Kate Sparrows is a Sassy Sue.

She's a cynical hopeless romantic that's in love with her Kindle and book boyfriends. It's really a love that you shouldn't come between. Well, unless you have ice cream, an awesome accent, or an amazing book in your hand. Bonus points having for all three.

Acknowledgements

I want to thank everyone for so patiently waiting for the rest of Jack's story. Some of you were more patient than others. It meant a lot to me that you reached out to offer me your thoughts while spreading news of my book and leaving honest reviews.

I want to thank Melody Pond again for another great book cover. She does wonderful work and I'm so glad that she continues to work with me.

I want to thank my boyfriend, Jorge. You nag me to keep writing. Well, you distract me 99.99% of the time and then lay on the guilt that I should be writing. Still, I guess you're kind of awesome.

And, of course, I want to thank everyone who is reading this right now. Without you, the stories would have no reason to leave my head.

www.ingramcontent.com/pod-product-compliance
Lightning Source LLC
Chambersburg PA
CBHW021042130626
46552CB00005B/1969